Dragon Flight

Books by Jessica Day George

Dragon Slippers
Dragon Flight
Dragon Spear

Sun and Moon, Ice and Snow
Princess of the Midnight Ball

Dragon Flight

Jessica Day George

BLOOMSBURY

NEW YORK BERLIN LONDON

Published by Bloomsbury U.S.A. Children's Books
175 Fifth Avenue, New York, New York 10010

The Library of Congress has cataloged the hardcover edition as follows:
George, Jessica Day.
Dragon flight / by Jessica Day George.—1st U.S. ed.
p.   cm.
Summary: Young seamstress Creel finds herself strategizing with the dragon king Shardas once again when
a renegade dragon in a distant country launches a war against their country, bringing an entire army of
dragons into the mix.
ISBN-13: 978-1-59990-110-7 • ISBN-10: 1-59990-110-2 (hardcover)
[1. Dragons—Fiction. 2. Kings, queens, rulers, etc.—Fiction. 3. Friendship—Fiction. 4. Fantasy.] I. Title.
PZ7.G293317Dr 2008   [Fic]—dc22   2007050762

ISBN-13: 978-1-59990-359-0 • ISBN-10: 1-59990-359-8 (paperback)

Typeset by Westchester Book Composition
Printed in the U.S.A. by Quad/Graphics Fairfield
7 9 10 8 6

For my own curious little monkey, who already loves books and whose naps made it possible for this one to be written

A Basin of Water

There are three truths I have come to learn in the year since the Dragon War. The first is that both humans and dragons have the capacity to be good or evil. The second is that even if you're doing something you love, you can still become bored with your work. And the third truth is that my business partner, Marta, will never be finished with her wedding gown.

Either one of them.

"It's so *white*," Marta complained for the thousandth time.

I tried to put my head in my hands, and nearly poked myself in the eye with a needle. I jerked back just in time, and glared at the needle. "Marta," I said.

"Yes?"

I had no idea what else to say, so I shook my head instead. My gaze fell on some blue fabric that lay on the cutting table in front of me. "Your gown for the Moralienin ceremony isn't white," I offered. Of course, we had had this conversation so many times that I knew exactly what was coming next.

"But that's a *set pattern*," she said, as she always did. "No room for us to experiment, to really make it special." She flapped her hands in agitation. "And I have to sew every stitch myself, it's tradition."

I put my needle down and ground the heels of my palms into my eyes. "Maaarta," I wailed.

"Oh, I'm sorry, does this *bore* you?" She threw a spool of thread at me. "Just because it's *my* wedding, and not yours!"

That hurt, but I didn't let it show on my face. I knew that Marta hadn't meant it to be mean. I had never confided my fears to her—that I would end up a lonely spinster, running the dress shop by myself after she was long wed. After all, I had had the audacity to fall in love with a prince, and princes do not marry shopkeepers.

"Don't worry, Creel, you'll be married soon enough." Alle, our assistant, came in with a bolt of cloth in her arms and a mischievous twinkle in her eye. I was sure she knew exactly what we had been talking about.

"No, I won't," I protested.

"You get more letters from Prince Luka than his father does," Alle said, unintentionally causing me another pang. "And he's supposed to be passing along information to the king about Citatie."

"Where is Citatie, anyway?" I asked in an attempt to change the subject.

I really did want to know about Citatie: I had never dared to tell Luka that I had no clue where he was. All I knew was that it was very hot there, and that their king was very odd. Although Luka and I were just friends—how could we be anything more than that?—I hated to look foolish in front of him. The schoolmistress in Carlieff Town, where I grew up, had been a bit vague about the geography outside of Feravel's borders.

"It's to the south, across an ocean," Marta said, sounding just as vague as my old teacher.

Alle shrugged. It seemed that we had all had the same level of schooling. I sighed.

"If you are done fussing over Marta's gowns, which needn't be finished for *four more months*," Alle said, "I believe that it's time to open the shop. The invitations to the crown prince's wedding were sent out two days ago; there should be quite a few wealthies wanting new gowns for the feasts and the ceremony."

"And that's another thing," Marta said as we took off our work aprons and straightened our hair in the mirror on the wall. "We're making the clothes for the royal bride-to-be, we're friends with both princes, yet where's our invitation to the wedding?"

"Marta," I said, even though secretly I was a little hurt by this as well as by their teasing, "we're commoners."

"Be that as it may," she said severely, "you're still the Heroine of the Dragon—"

I whirled around. "Don't say it," I told her. "Don't even think it. I own a dress shop and girls from small northern towns who own dress shops do not go to royal weddings. I'm not some mythical warrior woman."

That was what I told myself every day. King Caxel had once offered to have me marry Miles, as a reward for my part in the Dragon War, and I had refused. I truly had no desire to be a queen or a princess, but it still pained me that in refusing Miles I had cemented my status as a common merchant with no chance of becoming one of Marta's wealthies, who had the right to dance with princes.

Or to marry them.

Her eyes filled with sympathy as though guessing at my roiling emotions. We opened up the shop in silence.

My hurt deepened as the day wore on and just as Alle had predicted, customers poured in to demand gowns for the royal wedding. It seemed that everyone with the least title, the least bit of wealth, had been invited. But I *know* Crown Prince Milun, I cried out inside. Marta and I were among perhaps a dozen people who had permission to call him Miles. And yes, Luka and I could never be more, but we were friends, after all.

I steeled myself with the thought that Marta and I wouldn't have enough time to make ourselves new gowns, anyway. We had more than two dozen orders by the end of the day, and would have to hire temporary help to measure and cut the fabric. This was cheering, since it meant continued profit and success. If things continued in this manner, we would be able to take on a permanent apprentice or two in the next year.

By the time the shop closed I was exhausted. I didn't want to see one more ribbon or bolt of cloth, and I certainly didn't want to attend any feasts or ceremonies. But before I could lie down for some much-deserved sleep, I had one last thing to do.

In my bedroom above the shop I had two washbasins. One was painted with flowers and birds, and had a matching pitcher beside it. I washed my face and hands in it morning and night, and it was quite lovely. Across the room from this basin was a small table bearing another washbasin. This one was a heavy, gaudy thing, made of beaten gold and set with roughly cut crystals. There was always water in it, which I never changed.

The gold basin had come from the hoard of a dragon, and the water in it had been alchemically charged.

I pulled up a tall stool. Why stand when you can sit, as my mother used to say. I leaned my elbows on the table, one on each side of the basin, and yawned at my reflection.

"Lovely," rumbled a voice from the water.

During my yawn, the reflection of me looking tired had been replaced with the image of a large gold dragon.

Shardas the Gold had big blue eyes and blue horns, and the scales down his nose were so new and bright that they put the golden basin to shame. His horns, I noticed, were ragged and needed trimming.

"Sorry," I said. I yawned again; I couldn't seem to stop. "You look well."

"You look tired," Shardas said kindly.

"The invitations to Miles's wedding were just received," I explained. "All the wealthies need new gowns." The bitterness in my voice surprised me.

"Oh." He sounded disappointed.

"What's wrong?"

I wondered if he and his mate, Velika, felt snubbed. Of course, no humans but Luka, Marta, and I knew that Shardas and Velika were still alive, so it made sense that they wouldn't have been invited. They were believed to have died along with the horrid Princess Amalia of Roulain a year ago.

"I had thought that you might have time to visit us soon, but if you are busy . . ." He sighed, and it stirred the water. Seeing ripples form under the surface of the water was fascinating, and I thought about re-creating the image in embroidery.

Bringing my mind back to the present, I pursed my lips. "Hmmm. I *would* like to take a break from the shop," I said. "If I brought some pieces to embroider with me, I could do them at the cave. And we'll be hiring extra help, so Marta and Alle should be all right."

Shardas grinned, showing off his impressive teeth, and his tongue, which was the length of my arm.

"You look just like Azarte," I told him, naming the leggy hound that had once belonged to his cousin Feniul and now resided with Miles at the palace. "His tongue is almost as long."

Shardas pulled his tongue back in and rolled his eyes at me. "I will tell Feniul to fetch you from the usual spot at the end of the week," he said.

"Perfect."

"Bring a sheep."

"What?" I imagined trying to tie a bleating sheep to the back of Feniul, Shardas's dog-loving cousin. "Absolutely not. I'll bring you peaches and apples and perhaps some sweet figs. No live animals."

"Smoked ham?"

"Fine."

"And Velika likes sausages."

"Since they don't squeal and relieve themselves on my shoes, that sounds just fine as well."

"You were raised on a farm," Shardas reminded me with a laugh.

"Precisely why I now live in the city and have no livestock," I countered, drily. "If we get enough temporary help, I can stay for a week this time," I said.

"Excellent. We shall look forward to seeing you."

I smiled at my old friend, but I almost felt like crying. Shardas, I knew, did look forward to seeing me. But his mate was another story. She was more badly injured than he, and had not been well prior to their plunge into the Boiling Sea to stop Princess Amalia and her horrible dragonskin slippers. In the times I had visited Shardas and Velika, I had rarely seen her, and never heard her speak. I would bring her bushels of sausages if it would help, but I doubted that it would.

"Until the end of the week, then," I said warmly.

His image rippled and was replaced by my reflection. I slithered off the stool and went to bed.

By the Lake

T wo weeks later I was sitting on a rock on the shore
of a blue lake, coaxing a tune out of my wooden
flute, when Shardas came out of the cave to complain
about the noise. Luka had given me the flute and tried to
teach me to play it, but he had been sent away to Citatie
before our lessons had gone very far. Still, I didn't think
I sounded all that bad.

"Creel, please stop," Shardas rumbled. Living with
dragons, I had developed a pretty good ear for their
great, craggy voices, especially Shardas's. He was
amused, but also firm.

"I haven't finished this tune," I replied.

"Oh, that was a tune?" His voice was light with false
innocence.

Picking up one of the small gray pebbles from the
shore, I lobbed it at him, sticking out my tongue for good
measure. He batted it out of the air and lay down by my
boulder.

"It's not that I mind," Shardas said, "but Velika is
trying to sleep."

"Oh." Feeling guilty, I slipped the flute back into its satin bag and hung it from my belt. "Sorry."

"Quite all right," he said. "She said to tell you that someday you might be a passable musician, and at that time, you may play for her."

I smiled. "All right."

"Now, if you would be so kind?" He rolled so that his back was to me, showing off the patchwork of old and new scales along his spine.

"Of course."

I stood up on my boulder and leaned over his back. The burned scales, black and rough and brittle, were coming off in patches as smooth new scales grew underneath. It was horribly itchy, and dragons, like most humans, cannot scratch the middle of their backs. I was doing my part to help by pulling out the loose burned scales from the places Shardas couldn't reach. He did the same for Velika, since she couldn't bear to be touched by a human.

When Shardas dove into the Boiling Sea only seconds after Velika made the plunge with Amalia in her claws, his dive was so forceful that he touched the bottom of the Boiling Sea itself and had felt, in the searing pain of the burning, poisonous water, a touch of blessed cool.

A current of fresh water flowed into the Boiling Sea from an underground river. It soon blended with the poisonous minerals of the sea and heated to boiling point, but Shardas had come near to its source, and it gave him hope. With only a moment to act before the waters overcame him, he lashed out with his tail and found Velika. Wrapping his long, dexterous tail around her neck, he pulled her down to that cool portal and forced his way through a hole in the rock that seemed barely big enough to fit a creature half his size. Fighting the current and dragging Velika, Shardas made his way through a narrow tunnel and into an underground lake of deliciously cold, clean water.

Racked with pain, melted scales now cooling into stiff armor, he pulled Velika's head up so that she could breathe, though there was no shore for them to rest on. They dozed in the water for hours before Shardas found the strength to lead Velika up another underground river, where at last they found a cave large enough to allow them to sleep and heal.

By working their way through the caves that riddled the Feravelan countryside, they had eventually made their way here, far to the east, to this beautiful lake and secure hollow hill. To rest. To heal. To hide.

"Over to the left," Shardas directed me, and I snapped back to attention and moved to loosen the scales where he indicated. "Be as thorough as you can. Feniul will be here soon."

"I know."

Luka, Marta, Feniul, and I were the only ones in the world who knew that Shardas and Velika had not died in

the Boiling Sea. Unfortunately, we all also had obliga-
tions back home. Feniul had his collection of dogs to
care for, Marta and I had the shop, and Luka was abroad.
This meant that for long weeks, Shardas and Velika were
on their own, living off what food Shardas could scav-
enge, and at the mercy of any humans who might stumble upon them. The poisonous waters of the Boiling Sea
had extinguished their fires and they could not fly, for
the delicate membrane of their wings had been burned
away. It was growing back now, far slower than their
scales, and their wings had the look of poorly made lace,
but it would be a long while before they would be able to
take to the air. This thought hurt me almost as much as
seeing their burned, scarred bodies.

"I'll get these off before Feniul and I have to leave,
don't worry," I grunted, placing a knee against some of
the sturdier new scales on his back so that I had leverage
to pull off more of the dead ones.

When I had pulled the last of the loose scales from
his back I picked up a metal file. The tall spines that ran
along Shardas's backbone would not fall off and be
replaced like his scales; they grew slowly, like fingernails,
but I was gradually reshaping them and trimming off the
damage with the file. It was like giving a manicure to a
giant. I scraped the file across a spine in an upward motion,
gritting my teeth at the sound it made.

"Shall I leave the file, so that you can attend to
Velika's spines?"

"Yes, do," Shardas said, shaking his head as the grating sound irritated his nerves as well. He stretched out the wing on the side opposite me, gingerly, and I averted my eyes from the sight. "I wish she would come out during the daytime. The sunlight would do her good," he said, his fretful tone making him sound like Feniul.

"I can understand being afraid of being seen," I said. I also wondered if her eyes couldn't stand the light. She had lived in the caves beneath the royal palace for over a century prior to her dive into the Boiling Sea, so it would have surprised me had Velika not been sensitive to sunlight.

"I hoped that the window would cheer her," Shardas went on, scratching now at the scales under one forearm. "But she is still so apathetic."

The window had alerted Luka and I to the possibility of Shardas's being alive. He collected stained glass windows, and one had been stolen from a chapel not far from here a few months ago. The priest reported the theft to the king, in hopes of receiving money to replace the window, and Luka and I had set off in joyous pursuit of the thief.

"Does Velika like windows?" I asked. "Did she collect them as well?"

"Well, no," he admitted. "She liked—likes— glassware. Vases, goblets, and the like. But I didn't know how to find any of that for her."

"I'll see what I can do," I promised. I gave the spine I

was filing an extra hard rasp. "You should have told me sooner," I scolded.

He shuddered. "Yes, yes, I'm sorry. Don't—"

We were interrupted by yapping.

A tiny white dog came running down the pebbled beach, barking in excitement. She fearlessly ran right up Shardas's foreleg, her little claws clicking and scrabbling, skittered over his shoulder, and into my arms.

"Hello, Pippin," I said, and let her lick my chin before putting her down on Shardas's back.

Pippin half-ran, half-slithered down his haunches and onto the beach again, going to the mouth of the cave to peek inside at Velika before running along the shore in the direction she had just come from. We could now see Feniul, a green dragon, making his way along the pebbles with great care.

Dragon expressions are not easy to read because their faces are not as mobile as a human's. I had found (and I could say without boasting that I had more experience in this than any other human living) that to gauge their mood, you had to rely more on body language and voice than facial expression. So it was easy, even from a distance, to see that Feniul was displeased with the pebbly state of the beach. He had been here before, of course, and had made his displeasure known then as well. When he had brought me here a week ago, he had proposed that I make use of my time by sweeping up the pebbles, to which I had made polite, noncommittal noises.

"The footing here is so treacherous," he complained as he reached us. "I thought you were going to sweep the shore." He leveled an accusing glare at me.

"I haven't had time," I said innocently. "It's good of you to make the journey, Feniul."

He sniffed. "Well, I did promise to take you back to the King's Seat."

"Feniul," Shardas rumbled. "Creel could not possibly sweep the shore of a lake clear of pebbles. In a week or a month. What would be left if she did?"

"Dirt that wouldn't turn and skid under my claws," Feniul retorted.

Shardas made a sort of hooting, snorting sound, and I covered my laugh by ducking my head to continue scraping at his spines.

"I know you're all laughing at me," Feniul said in a huff. "And I don't care! We'll see who's laughing when you twist your ankles walking on these pebbles, missy!" He lashed his tail, sending the pebbles in question clattering across the beach.

"Velika is trying to sleep," I said, shushing him.

"Oh, forgive me." Feniul stilled his tail, his head lowered in contrition. "I brought some supplies," he told Shardas in a low voice. "A sheep and some peaches." He gestured back the way he had come, where I could vaguely see a large bundle, tied up in what looked like a fishing net.

"Thank you, Feniul," Shardas said.

A single sheep and a bushel of peaches would feed

them for only a day, if that. But still, I was also grateful to Feniul. This lake was isolated: there were no large farms where a few fruits would not be missed, there were no forests with boar or deer. Mostly they ate fish, which Shardas caught by dragging a net through the water, and occasionally berries from the bushes in the surrounding countryside. Dragons couldn't pick berries, so I harvested as many as I could during my visits and put them in the cool, dark cave. I had also brought all the cured ham and sausages that Feniul could carry, along with enough food for myself, so that I wouldn't burden Shardas with caring for me as well as for Velika.

"I must get back to my dogs," Feniul said anxiously. "Asta is about to have her puppies."

"Well," Shardas said, amused. "Do give the new mother my best."

"I will," Feniul said without a trace of irony.

"I'll just get my things, and pay my respects to Velika," I said.

Ducking back into the cave, I found my bundle of clothes and made sure the straps were tight. Then I walked quietly to the back of the cave. There, curled up on a pile of dried bracken and grasses, lay the queen of the dragons.

Velika Azure-Wing was blue, or she had been. The rich blue of her scales had dimmed in the years she had been confined to a cave beneath the New Palace by a dead king whose heirs lived obliviously in the stately halls above. Now those dull blue scales were discolored and deformed by her burns. Shardas was doing his best to feed her and to help her shed the ruined scales, but she had been exposed to the Boiling Sea longer than he, and she would not go out in the sun to spread her damaged wings and feel its soothing rays.

Thinking she was still asleep, I started to back away again, but her voice stopped me.

"Are you leaving us again, human maid?" Rough and low, even for a dragon, her voice scraped at my ears.

"Yes, Your Majesty," I said, my knees trembling. She had never spoken directly to me before. "I have to go back to the King's Seat." I made a little curtsy. It was not half as awkward as it would have been a year ago: I was used to waiting on royalty now, and could curtsy and bob with the best of them. "But I hope to return soon with supplies."

"That would be good. I worry about my mate, trying to find food when he is also unwell." A sigh rasped out of her muzzle.

"I worry about him, too." Feeling brave, I took a step closer to her. Even injured and curled up like a sleeping cat, the queen of the dragons was an awesome sight. "If Your Majesty would do a small favor, for me and for Shardas?"

She raised her head a few inches. "Yes?"

"Go outside from time to time? Into the sun? Perhaps in the evening, or at dawn, when it is not too bright. I think it would do Your Majesty good to see the sun and feel its rays. My mother always said that sunlight was the best tonic in the world." I clutched at the divided skirts of my riding dress, wondering how she would take this advice from a young uppity human.

"I shall think on it," the queen dragon said after a moment's pause.

"Thank you, Your Majesty," I said. I curtsied again. "Please excuse me. I shall return as soon as I may."

"Farewell." Her large eyes closed and I tiptoed out, shouldering my bundle as I passed it.

"Oh, and Creelisel?"

Velika's voice stopped me in my tracks. I hadn't known that she knew my full name.

"Yes, Your Majesty?" I had to squint to see her humped shape in the shadows.

"You may call me Velika."

The Countess's Trousseau

I think something purply down the front," Lady Isla said, waving her hand vaguely at the front of her skirt. She was standing in front of the full-length mirror in her room at the New Palace, trying on a gown for her bridal tour.

I looked over at Marta, who was crouched in front of the young countess, pinning the hem of the gown in question. Marta looked at me, eyebrows raised. The gown was pale yellow and would have green ribbons on the bodice and sleeves.

Putting down the wax tablet I had been sketching on, I walked over to the countess. Assuming a thoughtful expression, I circled her, tapping my cheek. "Hmmm."

"Don't you think that would be darling?"

Lady Isla was a beautiful young woman of eighteen, with soft brown hair and large brown eyes. Moreover, she was one of those fortunate people who can wear almost any color. Marta and I were in the process of designing and sewing the gowns for her upcoming marriage to Crown Prince Milun, which was a great honor for us, although somewhat stressful. If the future crown princess looked bad on her wedding day, the whole country would find out who had supplied her gown, and we would be ruined.

Lady Isla was from Dranvel, a county in the east of Feravel; she had been the ruling countess since her father's death just weeks after her twelfth birthday. She had never been to the King's Seat, preferring to stay on her estates, which she managed with an expert hand. Then when the capitol had been all but destroyed in the Dragon War the year before, Isla had come to the rescue, bringing men and supplies to aid in the rebuilding.

Dranvelan masons were known throughout the land for their fine work, and Dranvelan sheep were famous for their fine wool. Isla had brought skilled workers, fleece for new clothing, and the crop surplus from her lands, besides paying her taxes in advance to help restore the treasury. The result was that the New Palace was well on its way to being rebuilt, and Prince Miles had fallen madly in love with her.

And the normally sensible Isla, who had dressed all her life in sturdy, serviceable local wool with little color or ornamentation, had developed a sudden mania for high fashion and bright colors. She wanted her gowns for the wedding festivities to be the talk of the nation.

Adding to our mingled elation and anxiety was the process of dealing with the countess herself. While Isla was willing to listen to our advice, and more than willing to try on any daring creations we might suggest, she also had some suggestions of her own to make. And those weren't always the best.

Marta was much better at flattering our patrons than I, but since I had the reputation of being not only the Heroine of the Dragon War (which still made me wince), but also the genius behind the latest fashion for pictorial embroidery, I could get away with being blunt.

"You want to put purple embroidery on the front of a yellow gown with green ribbons?" I asked it calmly, as though merely clarifying the request.

"Yes." Isla's dark eyes flicked from the tall mirror before her to me. "Don't you think that would be simply stunning, Creel?"

"Well, you are correct, my lady, it *would* be stunning," I agreed. "But would it be stunning in a good way? *You* should wear the gown, not the other way around."

This had become a recent catchphrase of mine, faced as I was with the daily prospect of mousy women who wanted to wear cloth-of-gold, or older women who favored frilly pink gowns more suited to a young maiden. I had said it just a week before to a banker's young wife who asked us to sew real peacock plumes to the sleeves of a red gown, and her brow had puckered in confusion.

But Isla was not a light-minded banker's wife. She

pursed her lips, then gave a sigh. "You're right, that would be too much," she agreed.

"Perhaps a lighter shade of green, with emerald accents," Marta suggested, as though we hadn't already discussed this the day before. We had even brought the exact threads and ribbons with us today.

I snapped my fingers. "Perfect. My lady?" I cocked an eyebrow at Isla.

She looked at us, and then at her reflection, and a wry smile twisted her lips. She knew she had been manipulated into making the best choice.

"I'm sorry I even suggested it," Isla said as Marta helped her take off the half-finished gown. "I don't know what keeps coming over me: I have this constant urge to wear the brightest colors I can find. And to have gowns made from the most luscious silks and satins."

"No Dranvelan wool?" I gave her a sly look.

"None at all," she said firmly, and then she laughed. "I suppose I've just looked so drab all my life, and so has everyone around me, that when I came here . . ." She gestured from me to Marta. I was wearing a pale blue gown with dark blue and green ocean waves embroidered around the hem, and Marta was in cream with scarlet poppies winding around the skirt and up the sleeves.

I smiled at her, understanding. After years of hoeing potatoes and turnips, wearing threadbare gowns cut down from my mother's old clothes, I more than sympathized. Even the divided skirts I wore to ride horses—or

dragons—were of wool so fine it was like silk and embroidered with birds and clouds.

"We'll keep you in check," I said with a grin. "And
make sure that you look elegant and not . . ." I waved
my hand.

"Gaudy?" Isla suggested. "Make sure I don't frighten
horses and small children?"

We all laughed.

There was a knock at the door.

Marta helped Lady Isla into a quilted dressing gown
while I draped a length of linen over the yellow gown, in
case it was her betrothed at the door. It was unlucky for
the groom to see any of the trousseau, and poor Miles
had had enough bad luck in his young life.

"Enter," Lady Isla called when she had the dressing
gown fastened.

"Countess." The footman at the door bowed smartly.
"Mistress Carlbrun. Mistress Hargady." A nod for each
of us. "I have messages—for you, Lady Isla, and for Mistress Carlbrun." He held out two folded squares of vellum. One was unsealed, and had probably been written
here in the palace, and the other was sealed and looked
rather bent and grimy.

That was the one with my name on it.

"A note from Luka?" Marta's eyes twinkled as I took
the sealed letter. The footman's eyes widened at the
familiar way she referred to the younger prince.

"It looks like his handwriting," I replied, sliding a

stitch-ripping knife under the seal and unfolding the worn vellum. In truth I had recognized the dear, untidy scrawl at once, and my heart was fluttering.

I scanned the few lines of the letter quickly and then read them again. Dimly I heard Lady Isla dismiss the footman and ask Marta to help her dress. Dimly I heard Marta ask the countess what was the matter and dimly I heard the countess tell me that I was to accompany her to the council chamber to meet with the king.

Over and over again I read the letter, the words straggling slantwise across the page and blotted with ink. Luka had been in a hurry.

I could understand why.

"Creel, what's the matter?" Marta tried to take the letter from my hand, but I couldn't make my fingers let it go.

"Where is Citatie, Lady Isla?" I asked.

"What?"

"This country, Citatie, no one seems to know where it is."

"It's far to the south," Isla told me. "Across the Strait of Mellelie from Roulain."

"Oh," I said.

"What are you talking about? Creel? What's wrong?" Marta took my shoulders, peering anxiously into my face.

"Citatie has declared war on Feravel," I told her through numb lips. "Luka says they're going to trample Roulain on their way, and then destroy us."

Marta gasped, and I couldn't understand why. That wasn't even the bad part.

Lady Isla had gasped as well. "Prince Luka wrote that to *you*? But why? My note only said that there was trouble to the south, and to come to the council chamber with you right now."

I loosened my fingers and put the vellum into Marta's hands at last. "Their entire army is mounted on dragons," I said.

Counseling the King

A h, Mistress Carlbrun, our resident expert," King Caxel drawled as I entered the council chamber behind Lady Isla. I wondered what I had done to offend him this time. The last time we had spoken, I had refused his offer for me to marry Miles. Since then I had offended him from afar by spending too much time with his younger son—or so I had gathered from the blank-faced sevants sent to fetch Luka whenever he dared to visit me at the shop.

The king waved Isla and me to two chairs, one on each side of Miles. The crown prince gave me a smile and a nod, which I returned, and his betrothed pecked him on the cheek.

"Hello, Creel," the man on my other side whispered. The portly Duke of Mordrel and I were old friends. "Your gown is a wonder, as always." I smiled in reply, aware of the king's furious eyes on me.

"Well, I assume that Luka told you," King Caxel said.

I nodded. The others assembled at the council table

murmured at this, looking speculatively at me, but I ignored them. It was none of their business if Prince Luka chose to tell me such things.

"My younger son has demanded that you be made privy to this council," Caxel said, which explained the fury on his face. People did not demand things of the king.

I said nothing, since I didn't know what to say. The king looked almost as if he was waiting for an apology, and I didn't feel I needed to apologize.

The Duke of Mordrel swept to my rescue. "Well, it makes sense, sire. Of anyone in Feravel, Creel has the most experience in dealing with dragons."

"Indeed." The king gave me a calculating look. "And did you know anything about this?" He held up a long scroll. I presumed it contained information on the plans of the Citatian army.

"Only what Lu—Prince Luka told me in a letter I received moments ago," I said.

"What did that letter say?"

"It said that he was in Citatie, and had learned that the Citatians planned to conquer Feravel and any nation in between. And that their army was mounted on dragons."

The king grunted. I gathered that his information was the same. Steepling his fingers, King Caxel looked at me. "I believe that during and after the Dragon War, Mistress Carlbrun, you were adamant that the dragons did not want to attack us."

"That's true, sire."

"And that they did not help humans fight other humans, unless compelled by alchemy such as that of Milun the First's slippers."

"Yes, sire."

"Then why is the entire Citatian army mounted on dragons?" He slapped his hand down on the table with a crack. "According to my son, there are hundreds— *hundreds*—of dragons, each with a mounted soldier, flying practice formations over Citatie's capital city of Pelletie."

I sank back into my chair in shock. Hundreds of dragons? I doubted there were fifty in Feravel . . . thirty, perhaps. Where had Citatie found hundreds? And why were they helping the army?

"I—I don't know, sire. Perhaps their alchemists have done something. . . ." I let the sentence hang. Just because I talked with dragons a great deal didn't mean I knew everything about them. It made me uncomfortable to see a roomful of important men—a king, dukes, chancellors—all waiting for me to tell them what was happening.

"But you don't know that for sure," the king said. "They could be helping freely."

I shrugged, although the thought horrified me. "I . . . suppose. But it's very, very unlikely."

Earl Sarryck, the commander of the Feravelan army, spoke up. "I've told you time and again, sire, these creatures are dangerous."

I glared down the table at him. While Luka, the Duke of Mordrel, and I had been working during the war to protect the dragons from the power of Milun the First's slippers by putting alchemical collars on them, Earl Sarryck had decided it would be easier to "exterminate" them. It seemed that, even though the war was over and the dragons had faded into near-legend once more, he was still pushing to eliminate them.

"Earl Sarryck," I said, not bothering to keep the snap out of my voice, "have you ever killed a man?"

"I am the commander of the King's Army of Feravel, young woman," he snapped back. "I have done my duty."

"Then it might also be argued that you are dangerous, and should be exterminated. The dragons—"

"Creel," the Duke of Mordrel said in a soft voice, squeezing my hand. "Allow me to handle this." He looked at Sarryck, whose face had gone from red to purple at my words. "The dragons of Feravel are the greatest allies we have right now," he said. "Approaching them with violence will not help. We must persuade them to work with us, to help protect our borders from this threat."

"If these beasts can be persuaded to help." Sarryck snorted.

"These beasts?!" I started to rise to my feet, but the Duke of Mordrel's hand on my wrist stopped me.

"We need to find out what our dragons know," he said as I sank back down. "And see if they won't help us."

"Help us how?" King Caxel looked incredulous. "Citatie has hundreds of dragons, we have a double-dozen or so, which Mistress Carlbrun claims will not fight without alchemical coercion."

"No alchemy!" I burst out, and once again the duke squeezed my wrist.

"Perhaps not fight," he said. "But who better to spy on a dragon than another dragon?"

I opened my mouth in an "O." I hadn't thought of that. I had only been thinking of how best to defend my friends' honor, and how quickly I could get out of the council chamber. But spying . . . I instantly began to think of the dragons of my acquaintance and who would be best suited to the task, fiddling with the lacing of my cuffs as I thought. Feniul? Too nervous. Shardas was still wounded, and not opposed to being thought dead. Niva, a large female who had been of great help during the war, would make an excellent spy, but she did not care for humans or their politics.

Of course, this was a matter of dragons. . . .

"Mistress Carlbrun, are you even listening to me?"

Looking up from my cuffs, I saw that the king and his entire council were staring at me. King Caxel's eyes bulged unbecomingly, and I realized that he had been trying to get my attention for some time.

"I'll do it," I said.

"You'll do what?"

"I'll round up some dragons and lead a scouting

mission into Citatie." We could meet up with Luka and combine our information, I decided.

"You'll do nothing of the kind," King Caxel informed me. "While you were woolgathering, I was ordering you to assemble three dragons here tomorrow, so that the earl and his men might ride them to Citatie."

Sarryck spoke up. "There was a grayish sort of creature that I recall from the war. He seemed fairly manageable."

"Amacarin?" I raised my eyebrows. "Do you really think that Amacarin would give you the time of day? You killed his best friend."

"His 'best friend'?" Sarryck looked incredulous. "You believe these creatures form such attachments?"

"Yes, I do. And moreover, they have feelings and hold grudges, which is why I doubt I could get one of them to even speak to you, let alone allow you to ride him." I shook my head, turning to the king. "Your Majesty, if I am 'the expert' as you said when I entered the room, then you must allow me to do this my way. I will gather some dragons, and I will take them to Citatie. We will meet with Prince Luka, and see what we can discover."

"My younger son is hardly a trained spy," the king argued. "I need someone with experience on this mission."

"Very well, what about Tobin?" Tobin had been Luka's bodyguard until recently, when the king had allowed him to step down from active duty and take up a position training the Royal Guards. He was also betrothed to Marta, which is why the formidable warrior was to be found haunting a dressmaker's shop in the evenings.

The king started to argue again, but then stopped. "Tobin," he said thoughtfully, stroking his chin. "Just the man."

"Good." I looked at the large clock at the far end of the room. "He should be at my shop at this time of day. I'll tell him what we've decided, and we'll contact the dragons. Good day, Your Majesty." I swept out without asking permission, more worried about how I was going to convince Niva to help with human politicking than I was with a breach in etiquette. On my way through the halls of the palace, I collected Marta and our things, and went home to tell Tobin that he was coming with me to Citatie to spy on an army of dragons.

"You'd think the king would have been a bit more gracious," I muttered to myself as we carried the pieces of Isla's wardrobe into the shop. "After all, I offered to be tangled up in this. It's my neck that's sticking out."

Marta, whom I hadn't yet told about the council, looked at me wide-eyed. "Tangled up in what? Oh, Creel! What did you say to the king this time?!"

Persuading Dragons

As I had suspected, Niva was not easy to convince. She, Feniul, and Amacarin had agreed to meet me at a clearing near Feniul's cave in the Rath Forest, but neither Niva nor Amacarin looked interested in spying on the Citatians.

"It's clear what has happened," Niva said, buffing one of her talons with a rock. "The leader of the Citatians has a pair of dragonskin slippers and is using them to control the dragons. If we were to go there, we would fall under their thrall as well. Out of the question."

"We still have collars," I argued. "You would be protected." A stack of collars, woven from silk and infused with herbs and a special wax, resided in a chest in my room.

Niva shuddered, rattling the scales along her shoulders. "I did not particularly relish the sensation of being collared before, Creelisel. I plan on never repeating it."

"But what about the Citatian dragons?" I wheedled. "They need our help!"

"I don't know any Citatian dragons," Amacarin said. "I really don't care what happens to them."

"I don't know any either," I began, "but—"

"Then you should forget about it too," Amacarin said. He spread his wings prior to taking off.

"But I can't just forget about it," I protested. "What's happening there is wrong. And what's going to happen when they conquer Feravel? It will be your problem when they're standing outside your cave! When the Citatian king arrives with his slippers, and you start to feel the compulsion to obey him, you'll regret not having helped to stop it before it got out of hand."

"Perhaps," Niva said. "And when that happens, I will do my best to find you and accept a collar to fight the alchemy at work. But until then, good day." And she, too, got ready to fly.

"Cowards!" I shouted, clenching my fists. "Shardas would help."

"Shardas is dead," Amacarin said, and he leaped into the sky.

Opening my mouth, I started to tell them that Shardas was not dead, but Feniul nudged me in the back with his nose. I went sprawling face-first into the leaf-strewn grass. The incident had the effect of stopping Niva mid-takeoff, and she hovered over me.

"Creel, are you hurt? Feniul, what on earth were you trying to do?" Settling to the ground, she delicately lifted me to my feet with one foreclaw. "Just because we don't support human politics is no reason to be rude," she scolded him.

"I wasn't trying to be rude," Feniul protested. "I was just . . . it was purely an accident . . . and she, er, well . . ."

"Yes, yes, I'm fine," I said, straightening my gown and trying to brush the leaves out of my hair. "He was only . . . I mean, it was nothing." Feniul and I exchanged guilty looks.

Niva, no fool, sat back on her haunches and surveyed the pair of us through narrowed golden eyes. Her tongue flickered out, and she tilted her head to one side, her green scales gleaming in the sunlight that filtered down into the clearing.

"What do you two know? You clearly know something. Creel, you mentioned Shardas, and then Feniul shoved you into a pile of leaves."

"It was an accident," Feniul wailed.

"Why shouldn't I mention Shardas?" I put in. "He and I are friends."

"*Are?*" Niva's voice was soft.

I felt myself pale, and began to beat at my divided skirts as though they were on fire rather than just dirty. Feniul scraped long furrows in the soft earth with his talons, then pretended that he was just stretching.

"Shardas survived?" Niva's voice rasped with incredulity. "Where is he?"

"Well, they're still very weak," I said.

Flame shot out of Niva's mouth. I dodged to one side, and the tree behind me burned merrily. Without looking, Niva reached out and smashed it to the ground with her claws, smothering the flames.

"They? The queen, too?" The green dragon's great voice was hardly more than a whisper.

"They were very badly injured," I said.

"Take me to them."

"We're not supposed to tell anyone," Feniul dithered. "If we take her, then—"

I sucked in a breath and blew it out. "It's not like she's an enemy, Feniul," I said. I gestured to Niva's side. "May I?"

She lowered herself so that I could mount. "Feniul, lead us," she ordered.

He heaved a great sigh and gathered himself. "Shardas won't like it."

"I don't care," Niva said.

We flew to the lake where Shardas and Velika were hiding. Shardas himself was lying on the pebbled beach in the sun when we arrived. Looking up and seeing two dragons circling overhead, he crouched in a defensive position in front of the cave mouth. But after we landed and I hailed him, he relaxed. Slightly.

"Shardas the Gold," Niva said with deep respect. She bowed her head until the tip of her nose touched the shore.

"Niva Saffron-Wing." He nodded politely, but his

blue eyes were on me as I slithered off her back. "Creel." His voice held a welcome and a warning.

"I tried to stop them," Feniul fretted.

"I'm sure you did, Feniul. But Creel is hard to stop once she gets going," Shardas said. I was cheered by the trace of amusement in his voice.

"You need have no fear on my account," Niva said, very proper, as she always was. "I would not dream of revealing you to anyone."

"Thank you, Niva."

"Then why did you have to come?" Feniul was still shuffling around, snorting and looking upset.

"To see with my own eyes that our king lives." Her voice faltered. "And . . . our queen?"

"She is within," Shardas said, gesturing to the cave that he still guarded. "She does not receive visitors."

"Of course not." Niva's head bobbed in agreement, and I thought her eyes shone with happiness or something like it.

"May I ask how you came to reveal our . . . continued existence?" Shardas looked at me gravely.

It occurred to me that this was the best possible chance for me to gain draconic support for my mission. Shardas, though he did like to avoid humans, was intelligent enough to know when he needed to intervene in their affairs. Even if he wouldn't order Niva to help me, he might at least help to convince her that she should.

Drawing a deep breath, I told him everything that I knew about Citatie and their army. I told him about Earl Sarryck and his lust for dragon blood (an aspect that I had previously concealed from Niva and the others, as it might make them more reluctant to help the humans).

"So you see," I finished, "I need to gather some of our dragons, to help spy on the Citatian army before they attack Feravel." I looked hopefully at my old friend.

"No." Shardas's voice was flat. "I will never again put any dragon under my rule in a position to be coerced by alchemy." He leveled his sapphire gaze at me. "Nor should you meddle in these affairs, Creel. You are too young for such matters, and it angers me that your king would put you in a position of danger. You must stay far away from Citatie, even as my people shall."

Opening and closing my mouth like a landed fish, I stared at him. "But, Shardas! These other dragons—"

"We dragons are an independent race. It is for the Citatian dragons to break free or perish," he pronounced harshly.

"But if they attack Feravel?"

"We will withdraw."

"You can't just hide in the forest," I protested. "They'll find you, or the slippers or whatever they've got will force you out of hiding."

"Then we will leave Feravel," Shardas said. "Once Velika is able to travel, we will find a place that is safe."

"You're being selfish!" I shouted at him. "We need to help the Citatian dragons."

"And you're being foolish," Shardas roared back. "You're going to get yourself killed, and now you have no slippers to summon help when you are in danger!"

"You're both being foolish," Velika rasped from the mouth of the cave. "And exceptionally loud."

Feniul moaned and swayed on his feet, and Niva let out an exclamation. I took a step back, to get out of the way of all the emotional dragons. Shardas fanned his lacerated wings in surprise and concern as Velika came out of the cave. Her eyes, a beautiful sea green, were nearly shut against the light, even though it was an overcast day. The look on her face made Shardas move aside quickly, so that she could come all the way out of the cave and onto the beach.

"You were right, Creel," Velika said, squinting around. "It is good to feel the sun."

The weak sunlight made the patchwork of new and old scales on her side glitter, and her damaged wings looked like pale blue lace. She stretched her long neck, her muzzle pointed skyward, and then her legs and tail.

"Now," she said when she had settled, looking at each of us in turn, "we have the matter of the Citatians to deal with."

Feniul seemed to be on the verge of fainting, and Niva looked torn between bowing and fainting herself. Realizing that I was fiddling with my skirts in a sort of half-curtsying fashion, I forced myself to stop. Shardas saw me straighten and smiled. I wrinkled my nose at him.

"The Citatians are coming to Feravel specifically?" Velika asked me.

"Yes . . . Velika." I heard Niva hiss at my use of the queen dragon's name. "They said they would destroy us, and anyone who stood in their way."

"I see." She looked thoughtful. "Has your king done anything to offend them?"

"He says not."

"Do they give any reason?"

"No."

"Odd." She reached up and scratched at a loose scale on the side of her neck. It fell to the pebbled ground with a clatter, showing a fresh patch of darker blue scales beneath. "We must find out how these dragons are being controlled, and why they are coming to Feravel."

"It does not concern us," Shardas said.

"It most certainly does," Velika argued. "They may be far away from here, but they are still our people. I would go myself, but I am too weak. And you cannot fly," she reminded Shardas, her voice compassionate. "It will have to be Niva and Feniul. Also, anyone else you can locate. Theoradus would be a good choice."

"I'm sorry, ma'am, but he's dead," I told her.

"Dead?" She looked sorrowful. "When?"

"Last year, during the war. He was shot down by arrows just before you, er, dove into the Boiling Sea."

"Ah." She paused. "Amacarin?"

"We spoke with him and he was quite reluctant to leave his home," Niva said, for all the world as though she hadn't refused as well.

"Tell him that he is ordered to go and give Creel whatever assistance is required," Velika said.

"Yes, Azure-Wing," Niva said.

"And you will go, too, of course, and Feniul."

"Me?" Feniul looked horrified. "But—but who will bring you sheep and things?"

"Is Leontes still alive?" Velika looked at me, but I shrugged. I had never heard the name.

"Yes, Azure-Wing," Niva said. "But my mate is occupied in guarding our hatchlings, far to the west."

"You have children?" I stared at her. I could not imagine the militant Niva as a mother, but I was less surprised to find that her mate watched their young.

"How many hatchlings have you?" Velika looked at Niva with interest. So did Shardas and Feniul. I wondered if they, too, were startled by the idea of Niva as a mother.

"Four," Niva said with no little pride. "All the eggs hatched."

"Wondrous," Velika said. "Can they fly yet?"

"Yes, Azure-Wing."

"Then have Leontes fly them here, to our cave. He will help us until we are healed. And the little ones will enjoy the lake." Her tone was almost wistful when she spoke of the "little ones."

"Yes, my queen." If Niva was irritated by this order to move her family across the country, she didn't show it.

Velika turned to me again. "What other humans will help you?"

"Prince Luka, whom you remember brought me here the first time," I said. "And a Moralienin sword master named Tobin."

"You trust this Tobin?"

"Yes, indeed. He's a very good man," I assured her. "He's engaged to my friend Marta," I added unnecessarily.

"Will he keep our secret?"

"Tobin is a mute, and the trusted companion of Prince Luka," Feniul said, which surprised me, since Feniul had never seemed to notice any other humans but me. I hadn't known that he even remembered Tobin's name.

"Excellent. Now go," Velika said. "Establish a speaking pool in Citatie as soon as you arrive, Niva, and report to us. I expect Leontes and your hatchlings within the week." She walked closer to the edge of the water and lay down. "Shardas and I will sleep now," she announced, dismissing us.

As I climbed onto Feniul's back, I saw Shardas lie down beside his mate, entwining his tail with hers. He saw me looking, and shot out a small spurt of blue flame in farewell. I waved, and Feniul took to the sky with a subdued Niva on his heels.

Winging Away

"You'll need a sweater, Tobin," Marta said, trying to jam a large wool pullover into his neatly packed bag.

Tobin and I exchanged rueful looks, and he made some gestures with his hands.

"I know it's warm there, but what if there's an unseasonable chill?" Marta stuck out her lower lip.

"Marta," I said cajolingly. "Tobin has been to Citatie before. If he wanted a sweater, he would have packed a sweater."

Marta tossed the sweater aside. "Fine!" She folded her arms, looking red and angry. "Of course *you* can be all cavalier about this, Creel. You're going to see your . . . Luka. I'm sending Tobin off to face who knows what! I have to sit here and sew and pretend that nothing's wrong for I don't know how long!" She was on the verge of tears.

Tobin went over and put his arms around her, and I busied myself packing my own things. We were in the living quarters over the shop. Niva, Amacarin, and

Feniul would meet us outside the city gates at dawn. Marta and I had been up all night, sorting clothes, packing hampers of food, and the like, but once Tobin arrived she had become increasingly nervous and demanding.

I could hardly blame her. It was true: I was concerned about Luka and it was a comfort to me that I would be with him in a matter of days. Marta and Tobin were to be married in the autumn, first here in the King's Seat, and then in Moralien (Tobin was not a believer in the Triune Gods, and so they were to be married twice to make both families happy). For all Marta knew, we would be gone until winter, or next summer, and the weddings would be canceled. For all Marta knew, we wouldn't come back at all.

While Tobin soothed her, I finished stashing my riding dresses in a large leather duffel bag. They would be sadly creased, but there was nothing I could do about it. My greater concern, beyond the threat of a second Dragon War, of course, was that Marta and our assistants would not be able to finish Lady Isla's trousseau in time for the royal wedding. On the other hand, if we were unable to avert this war, there might not be a royal wedding.

It was a sober party that rode out from our shop. Marta had, at the last minute, decided not to see us off at the site of the dragon rendezvous, and so we all hugged and kissed on the step of the shop. One of the King's

Guards accompanied us to the city gates. He would take the horses back to the royal stables and report our departure to the king. We rode in silence to a field outside the King's Seat, and waited until Niva, Amacarin, and Feniul arrived.

"I'm sorry, I'm sorry," Feniul apologized as the horses reared and snorted.

Tobin and I quickly handed our reins to the soldier, and sent him to wait some distance apart. I wanted to send him back to the palace entirely, to spare the poor horses any further distress, but he was under orders to see us fly away.

"What did you do with your dogs?" I asked Feniul, to lighten the mood while Tobin tied our bags and hampers to the dragons.

"Well, I took some to Shardas. He said that Niva's hatchlings can help care for them," Feniul told me. "And that nice Prince Milun has a few of the larger ones."

"He does?" This was rather startling. I didn't know that Feniul and Miles were friendly, although Feniul had given Miles a dog after the Dragon War.

"Yes, he and Azarte were hunting near my cave yesterday, and I asked him if he would take some of the larger dogs. Azarte will enjoy the company, I'm sure."

"I'm sure," I echoed. It was, I thought, a great step forward in human-dragon relations that the crown prince and Feniul could meet casually and do each other favors like this. "Take that, Earl Sarryck!" I thought.

"Are you quite ready?" Niva seemed anxious to be off, and Amacarin had hardly said two words to us. He looked slightly stunned, and I guessed the news that both Shardas and Velika were still alive had been a bit much for him to take in.

"Yes, I think so." I looked to my human companion. "Tobin?"

He nodded, and I started to climb up Feniul's shoulder. It was more comfortable for me to ride Feniul, first, because I knew him best, and second, because his neck was narrower than Niva's. Tobin was just settling himself on Niva's shoulders when another horse came galloping up.

"Wait!" Marta scrambled off the horse, dragging a large, overflowing leather knapsack with her. "Wait for me!"

"Caxon's bones," I swore. "What does she think she's doing?"

I looked over at Tobin, but he was already off Niva's neck and striding toward Marta. Her horse spooked and ran, and the soldier hovering at the edge of the field barely managed to catch it. Tobin grabbed Marta's arm, but she shrugged him off.

"Are you Amacarin?" She looked up at the blue-gray dragon, ignoring both Tobin's attempts to speak to her through hand signals and my continued profanity.

"Yes, I am." Amacarin looked down his nose at her. "Who are you?"

"I'm Marta," she said. "And I want to go to Citatie with you."

"It's all the same to me," Amacarin said. "Fasten that bag behind the other one on my back, and climb on."

"You're not helping," I said to him.

"Shardas ordered me to take some humans and spy on the Citatians," Amacarin said. "He didn't say how many humans, and frankly, we can use the help. Although I don't see what good a single human maid will do." He paused and looked at me. "You managed to cause quite a storm last time around, however."

Tobin looked at me, helpless in the face of Marta's stubborn determination. I shrugged.

"I guess Alle and the others will have to finish Isla's trousseau on their own," I said, half-resigned and half-hoping that the reminder of our royal commission would bring Marta around.

"Isla's trousseau can go to the bottom of the Boiling Sea for all I care," Marta retorted. She kissed Tobin's cheek and clambered up onto Amacarin's back to fasten her bag. "We can go in two minutes."

"Whenever you're ready," I sang out, and got back on Feniul.

Tobin, who appeared to be mouthing something that I was glad I couldn't hear, remounted Niva and sat looking into the distance while his betrothed scrambled about on the back of her dragon. It was some ten minutes before she was settled, and then we took off with the sun climbing the sky and the horses panicking below us.

I prayed to the Triunity for help as we winged our way toward Citatie and its army of dragons.

Heat That Shimmers Like Silk

The summers in Feravel could be very hot. In fact, most of my childhood had been characterized by droughts that dried up streams and withered crops. But I had never experienced heat like that in Citatie. The air wavered with it, and the sun on my head was tangible, like a weight pressing me against Feniul's neck. He and the other two dragons glided through the thick, dry air, moving their wings as little as possible. It seemed that even dragons were not immune to the heat.

"It's so horribly hot," Marta shouted to me.

I looked over at her. The neck of her riding gown was unfastened and she was fanning herself with a handkerchief.

Not wanting to open my mouth to shout back, for fear that the heat would dry up my tongue, I just fanned myself with both hands in agreement. Then I unlaced the sleeves of my gown and rolled them up, to get a bit of air on my arms. It was so hot I thought I might be sick.

"I feel as though I could set fire to the entire country," Amacarin announced. "How marvelous."

"My wings feel brittle, though," Feniul said. "I'm not sure the added fire is much compensation."

"You will both adjust to the weather," Niva said. "Now, Creel, where are we to meet this prince?"

"There is a large, flat-topped hill to the southwest," I said, remembering the directions Earl Sarryck had given me. It seemed that the Feravelan spy forces had a regular hideout here in Citatie. "On the north side is a cave entrance concealed by a grove of olive trees."

By the time we identified the correct plateau, in a barren landscape broken by many such broad, flat-topped hills, I was ready to faint from the heat. A glance at Marta showed that she was holding fast to the straps that held her baggage in place, as though that alone was keeping her to her seat. Tobin, stalwart as always, showed no sign of discomfort.

When Feniul came to rest on the shady side of the plateau, I all but fell off his neck and sat there beside an olive tree, panting for breath. Tobin dismounted with greater ease and went immediately to Marta to help her down. Her face was red and her strawberry-blond curls were bedraggled.

"No wonder they want to conquer Feravel," she gasped after drinking from the waterskin Tobin brought her. "It's too hot to breathe here, even in the shade."

Meanwhile, Amacarin was amusing himself by sending out little tongues of flame along the rocks and fallen branches of the olive trees. Feniul kept spreading his wings and checking them for signs of damage, and Niva watched them both with half-lidded eyes and an expression of disdain.

"Please put out that fire, Amacarin," I said. "It's hot enough without you setting the grove alight."

"Besides, you'll burn down the cover for the cave entrance," someone said from behind us.

"Luka!"

Smiling, the prince came out from behind another tree. He was very brown, and his hair had been cropped short. My heart lurched at the sight of him, and I went to give him a friendly hug, conscious of the others watching. I tripped over a tree root on my way and practically threw myself into his arms.

"Hello," I said, blushing bright red as I disentangled myself. "So nice to see . . . you're looking well."

"Hello." He was blushing, too.

Marta scrambled to her feet, and swayed in place until Tobin picked her up. He and his former charge—he had been Luka's bodyguard for years—exchanged nods.

Luka greeted the dragons, and then showed them how to walk around the grove to the cave entrance, which was large enough even for Niva to use. They had to lower their heads and tuck in their wings, but they followed us into the darkness without complaint. The entrance tunnel turned sharply before opening into a large chamber lit by torches. There were several Feravelan soldiers there, sitting on cots playing cards.

"I thought you'd be arriving soon, so I went to have a look," Luka explained, and then introduced the soldiers to us. I moved away from Luka, worried that one of the soldiers would report to King Caxel if we seemed too close.

The dragons settled themselves against one wall and the humans all sat on cots near the other, and there we were. The cave was hot and stuffy, not nearly as nice as Shardas's old lair, and with the dragons inside, it was barely large enough for us all.

"Well," Luka said after a moment, "here's the situation. King Nason will not back down. He actually ordered me killed, right there in his throne room." Luka's voice rose with disbelief. "So much for being a goodwill ambassador. If my men hadn't helped me escape out a window, I'd be dead."

My hand rose to my throat and my stomach knotted at the casual way Luka described his near murder. I gave him a quick look up and down, to reassure myself that he had escaped unscathed. He saw my look and squeezed my other hand. I caught one of the soldiers watching, and pulled my hand away.

"Shouldn't you have gone home, then?" Marta glanced around, nervous. "We're so close; I could see the city before we landed."

Luka shrugged. "Our spyhole hasn't been discovered yet. It seems safe enough: we're ten miles out and I doubt they suspect I'm still in the country."

"An excellent ploy, Your Highness," cheered one of the soldiers.

"So now what do we do?" It was Marta who voiced what I had also been thinking. Here we were in a foreign—and hostile—land with three dragons in tow. What next?

"Tobin and I are going to wear these Citatian uniforms and have the dragons help us infiltrate their army," Luka said. From under his cot he pulled a bundle that proved to be two white uniforms.

"What about us?" I said, gesturing to myself and Marta. "We're not just going to sit here all day."

Out of the corner of my eye, I saw one of the soldiers smirk and whisper something to the man nearest to him, but I ignored that. I hadn't come this far to hang back and let Luka and Tobin do all the work. And where dragons were involved, I felt I owed it to Shardas to do all I could to help.

"Don't worry, Creel," Luka said breezily. "I know you, and I know there's no way you'll hide here and let us have all the fun." He laughed, but Tobin made a face as if to say that there was nothing fun about it. "I bought you these." He reached under his cot again and pulled out a basket. It was full of garishly colored silk. "Some Citatian clothing. You can roam the marketplace to your heart's content, asking questions and listening to the latest gossip."

This made Marta frown. "We don't speak Citatian, though. Won't people know we're from Feravel?"

Luka shrugged. "Pretend you're from Roulain, or Moralien. Citatians love to shop, but there's some ancient law that says only one hundred Citatian merchants can set up shop at any given time, so they invite foreign merchants to Pelletie to fill the market."

I stared at him. For the thousandth time, I wished that the Carlieff schoolmistress had been a better teacher. There were more than one hundred dressmakers alone in the King's Seat. How was I supposed to help stop a war if I didn't know the first thing about our enemy's customs?

"What?" Marta was staring at Luka, too.

He laughed. "Oh, yes. Merchants from all over the world are invited to the Grand Market to hawk their wares for the Citatians' enjoyment. The visiting merchants' wives do a good deal of shopping as well, buying silks and jewels for themselves while their husbands try to turn a profit. The Citatians who have a merchant's license wear blue hats, but all the other merchants are foreigners. Take two soldiers with you as bodyguards, and you'll just look like some wealthy merchants' daughters."

Marta's eyes gleamed at this. "I think we can do that," she said, pulling some of the clothing out of the basket to look at it. "Wait a minute, what are these?"

Luka grinned at us both. "Haven't you ever seen Citatian fashions before, Marta? Creel?"

We both shook our heads. I held up more of the clothing, and my eyes bulged.

"Those are your new trousers," Luka said with a snicker. "Don't you like them?"

And now Tobin had a gleam in his eye. He smiled broadly while Marta and I both turned beet red.

Trousers!

A Shopping Spree

I feel so immodest," Marta hissed. "Do you think everyone is looking at us?"

"No." I shook my head, liking the feeling of the dozens of tiny braids swinging around my face. "There are plenty of women here dressed like this. Now stop fussing."

I, for one, was enjoying the Citatian mode of dress for women. The lightweight trousers were paired with a long tunic, belted by a sash that was wrapped from just under the bust to the top of the hips. Over that was a long loose vest, and a gauzy scarf worn loosely around the neck. Marta and I had braided each other's hair in a double-dozen tiny braids, tied with bright yarn. My straight hair had never looked so exciting, but Marta's curls were threatening to spring loose at any moment.

I did feel like the soldiers escorting us were looking at our legs a bit too much, but there was precious little I could do about that, so I chose to ignore it. I also chose to ignore the dragons flying endless formations overhead, since no one else was looking up. It was unnerving, but we didn't dare draw attention to ourselves by gawking.

What I didn't want to tell Marta was that I wasn't so much concerned about whether or not it was immodest to wear trousers, but with how the Citatians would receive us. Luka had assured us that the Grand Market was always full of foreign women, and that we would only be two more wealthy shoppers in the crowd. I couldn't help but remember my first day in the King's Seat, however.

Dowdily dressed, I had been looking for work at a dressmaker's shop, asking directions of strangers and wandering the streets until curfew. I had stepped on a small dog (Feniul's Pippin), and nearly caused a diplomatic incident with a Roulaini princess, the evil Amalia. I had been jeered at, ignored, and threatened with prison for violating a curfew I hadn't known existed. If our experience here in the Grand Market was at all similar, I didn't know what I would do.

All around us were Citatian men with tanned faces and pale hair, wearing conical red or purple or yellow hats, depending on their occupation. Every so often we saw a blue hat worn by someone working at a booth. Women in bright silks strolled in pairs with bare-chested bodyguards at their heels. The women held square sunshades to keep their skin from being tanned like their husbands', and their pale braids were often dyed fanciful colors: royal blue, scarlet, and deep green.

But there were also women and men with tattooed hands wearing dark robes, shoppers in high-collared, lace-trimmed Roulaini gowns and suits, and some people wrapped head to toe in long, seamless draperies that left one shoulder bare. Many of the women had small pet monkeys with jeweled collars frolicking along beside them, attached to their mistresses by long chains that fastened to a bracelet on the women's wrists.

"We should get a monkey," Marta said. "It seems to be the accessory of choice."

"Absolutely not," I disagreed. "Don't you remember Lady Katta's pet monkey? It shredded two of her gowns with its little fingernails, and when she scolded it, it flung its own waste at her!"

Marta made a face. "Bleah. I'd forgotten that."

We went to a booth that sold bolts of silk embroidered with tiny silver mirrors. Far from sneering at us, the proprietress scrambled to show us her finest wares, bowing and smiling and communicating to us in broad gestures. She wore mirrored silk twisted and draped around her stout figure, leaving both arms and one shoulder bare. I was hard-pressed not to stare at the tattoo of a snake on her naked shoulder.

While the merchandise was appealing, it was clear that she spoke not a word of Feravelan or Roulaini, which I knew a few words of. Marta also tried Moralienin, Tobin's native tongue, but got nothing more than nods and smiles. Still, I resolved to come back another time and buy a bolt of the mirrored silk. It would be a wondrous addition to Isla's trousseau. We would just have to look elsewhere for someone to gossip with.

It was Marta who spotted a trio of Moralienin men coming out of a low building near some leather workers. Their shaved heads and gold earrings hardly looked exotic in the sea of strange clothing that we were walking through, but people gave the heavily armed, fierce-looking men wide berth nevertheless. Marta immediately took my arm and dragged me within earshot of them, much to our bodyguards' horror. As we strolled by with false casualness, Marta began to jabber in Moralienin, while I nodded and smiled as though I understood every word.

The ploy had the desired effect, and one of the burly men stopped in surprise. Addressing Marta, he bowed to us and then apparently introduced himself and his men. Marta introduced herself using Tobin's sister's name, Ulfrid, and then called me something that sounded like "Hime-trout."

Releasing my arm to gesture effusively, she chattered (as near as I could tell) about the market and the strange clothes and then grinned broadly, seeming to invite the men to add their own opinions. I groaned inwardly. Tobin and his sister were so taciturn that I had thought Ulfrid was also mute when we first met. I couldn't imagine that these men would really believe us to be their countrywomen, the way Marta was babbling on.

Much to my surprise, the men were excited to hear their mother tongue and replied with equal fervor. They went on at some length, with Marta and me nodding and smiling and me hoping ardently that Marta understood. Then Marta started up again, and judging by her flapping arms, she was talking about dragons.

The Moralienin men all nodded gravely. Then they bowed and walked away, leaving us standing with our bodyguards in the middle of an empty space in the market.

"Well." She put her hands on her hips. "How rude!"

"I'm guessing that they didn't want to talk about all the dragons flying overhead," I said in a low voice.

"Apparently not," Marta said, still sounding put out. Then she bit her lip. "How was my accent, though? Did it sound like theirs?"

"Marta, we're trying to stop a war with the Citatians." I pointed at the dragons flying above us. "Remember?"

"Yes, but when this is all over, I have to meet Tobin's mother, and then recite my lineage in Moralienin, and I'm nervous."

"Don't worry," I said with false cheer. "If we don't find someone to talk to us soon, you'll never have to meet Tobin's mother. We'll all be dead."

She punched me in the arm. "You're horrible."

"Gaal matto!" A Citatian man in a merchant's blue hat shoved a monkey between us. "Gaal matto?"

"No monkeys!" I shook my head emphatically. "We don't want a monkey!" Then I got a good look at him. "You!" I rudely pointed my finger right in his face. "You lived in the King's Seat! I saw you!"

On my unfortunate first day in the King's Seat, shortly before stepping on Pippin, I had been asking directions to the cloth-workers' district. I was certain this was the same man I had first asked, but he hadn't spoken Feravelan. Still, that had been almost two years ago.

"You," I said again. "Remember me?" I pointed to my chest. "Where is the cloth-workers' district?" I smiled and nodded. "Then, little dog, bark, bark, and princess." I waved my hands around my head to indicate lots of curly hair. Meanwhile, Marta and our bodyguards were staring at me as if I'd grown two extra heads.

"Ah, pretty maidy! Hello!" The monkey seller beamed at me. "Little dog, woof, woof!" He laughed like a maniac. "Little dog, pretty maidy, mean maidy. Pretty maidy buy monkey?" He brandished the little black-and-white creature on his arm in my face.

"No, no monkeys," I said, but I smiled while I said it. I reached out and stroked the monkey's head. It was quite a darling, really, mostly black with a wild mane of white hair. Then I thought of Lady Katta's pet and withdrew my hand. "Why are you here?" I opened my arms to show puzzlement, then pointed to the ground.

"Ah." He nodded. "Dragons, much fire, whoosh,

whoosh!" He blew out his cheeks and flapped his arms, nearly flinging the monkey into Marta's face. "Monkeys all go, poof." It wasn't clear if they were killed, or if they simply fled in terror, but his smile didn't waver so we continued to smile back. "Come home, wives happy, mother happy. Buy monkey?" He thrust the creature at Marta, who took it and held it at arm's length.

"But dragons *here*," I said, waving both hands in the air. "Many more dragons."

"Hee-hoo," the monkey seller said, rolling his eyes and flapping his hands. "Dragons here good. Fly all day, lay eggs, eat bad dogs. Not burn houses. Nice dragons."

"Oh, yes, very nice," I said. Behind me, one of the soldiers snorted and I put my hand behind my back and snapped my fingers for him to be quiet. "But why do the dragons want to burn Feravel?"

He threw up his hands in ignorance. "King angry?" He turned his attention to Marta. "Monkey like you. You buy."

The monkey had crawled up Marta's arm and was busy unraveling one of her braids. "Er, all right." She pulled some coins out of her purse and handed them to the man. "Thank you."

"Nice, nice, pretty maidies," the monkey seller said in delight, and then trotted a few paces away to a booth where there were cages with more monkeys and a few exotic birds. He put the coins in a carved box, guarded over by a hook-nosed woman a foot taller than he.

Another equally broad-shouldered and grim woman sat by knitting.

"Which one is his wife?" Marta whispered as we smiled and nodded and strolled away.

"Probably both," I said. "He said 'wives happy.' Luka told me it's the fashion to have at least two."

"Ugh. I wouldn't allow Tobin to have another wife," she said.

"I'm not sure I want *one*," the soldier behind Marta said. We both glared over our shoulders at him.

"Why do you think the king is so angry at Feravel?" Marta asked, freeing her hair from the monkey's grasp and moving him to the crook of her elbow.

"Let's ask him," I said. I went back to the first booth we had stopped at, the one that sold mirrored silk.

It was quite exquisite. The silk itself was heavy and slick, almost like satin but with a luscious depth to the color. The mirrors were tiny bits of polished silver, sewn into the fabric with silk thread.

Marta jostled my elbow. "Ask him? You mean the king?"

"Yes. No use dancing around the cart when you want a ride, as my mother used to say. Just hop in and whistle."

Using my fingers and a range of exaggerated facial expressions, I had the beaming woman cut several yards in red, gold, and green silk. I pulled the Citatian coins Luka had given me out of my belt pouch, and laid them on the table one at a time until the woman nodded, satisfied.

Marta watched me buying cloth with a stunned look. "How do you plan to ask the king?"

Complacent, I gathered up my purchases, now safely wrapped in coarse broadcloth. "First we're going back to our cave to do a little sewing, and then I'll show you," I told her. "But if that monkey ruins anything . . ." I let my voice trail off meaningfully.

"I hear that you can eat monkey," one of the soldiers supplied.

"Delicious," I said.

Linen Bandages and Mirrored Silk

Back at the cave, Marta shrieked in horror as I proceeded to cut the mirrored silk into long strips. "Creel! What are you doing? You're ruining it!"

"Just wait and see," I said. When I had made several long ribbons out of the edges of the mirrored cloth, I opened my baggage and pulled out a blue satin riding dress. With a pang, I started to cut the divided skirt free of the bodice.

"Now I know you've gone insane," Marta said. Her hands fluttered, as though she was debating snatching the gown away before I did any more damage.

There was a scuffling and the sound of voices at the mouth of the cave, and Luka and Tobin came in with a soldier and the dragons hard on his heels. "Luka," Marta appealed to him. "Creel's gone mad; you have to speak to her."

I looked up to assure Luka that I hadn't, suppressing a thrill of delight at being near him again, and saw the expression on his face. I cast aside my work. "What happened?" Then I saw that there were only two dragons with them, and my heart shuddered. "Where's Niva?"

Marta gasped and ran to embrace Tobin, whom I now saw had a long cut down the sleeve of his white Citatian uniform. Red stained the edges of the cut, but he seemed calm enough. Of course, he always seemed calm.

"Female dragons do not fly in formation here," Luka said.

He helped Marta strip off Tobin's tunic so that she could look at his arm. There was a long, shallow cut on his forearm, but it looked like it wouldn't need stitching. We all breathed a sigh of relief and Marta set about washing the wound.

"I had no idea," Luka went on. "I can't tell the difference between a male and a female unless I hear them talk."

"Neither can I," I admitted.

"We were flying above the city and a half dozen other dragons surrounded us. The soldiers have brass trumpets, to make their voices louder. I tried to steal some when I took the uniforms, but I couldn't. Anyway, the soldiers started to shout to us: why did we have a female, where were her eggs, who was our commander." Luka made a face. "What were we to do? My Citatian is fairly good, but it was hard to keep my accent correct while I was shouting. I told them that we had orders from Commander Toukas, the only commander whose name I know, and they followed us all the way to the palace."

Luka sat down on a cot and began rubbing his face. He yanked off the spiked steel helmet he wore with his uniform and threw it on the floor. "We landed in the courtyard behind the palace, where the royal dragons land. Toukas himself came out to meet us. He recognized me at once and shouted for the guards. We started to take off again, but the dragon patrol threatened to burn us. They threw a net over Niva, saying something about her being uncollared."

"Didn't she have her collar on?" I checked Feniul and Amacarin, and they were both collared. We had put the alchemical creations on all three dragons before leaving Feravel, just to be safe.

"She did, but the Citatian collars are leather—ours don't pass muster. Tobin cut himself free of the net, and tried to make the hole larger for Niva. But you know how she is: she started shouting that we should go, go at once. Feniul snatched up Tobin and we fled. It took two hours of some pretty fancy flying before we lost them and decided it was safe enough to come here."

Feniul leaned in. "I'm sorry about your arm," he said to Tobin. "Is it bad?"

Tobin shook his head as Marta bandaged it with some linen one of the soldiers gave her.

"Scraped him with a claw?" I patted Feniul's foreleg. "I'm sure it was an accident."

"Of course it was," Amacarin said haughtily. "And isn't anyone going to ask what my human and I discovered?" The soldier standing beside the blue-gray dragon looked disgruntled at being called Amacarin's "human."

"You weren't with them?" I asked at the same time that Luka said, "Sorry. What *did* you find?"

Amacarin puffed out his gray-blue chest. "We found a *massive* hatching ground," he announced, clearly expecting an impressive reaction.

He got it, but from Feniul alone. We humans just looked puzzled.

"Oh, my! How many hatchlings did you see?" Feniul's eyes gleamed, and he lashed his tail in excitement. "A dozen? Any sign of other eggs?"

"A dozen?!" Amacarin snorted in disdain, nearly setting my sewing afire. I pulled it out of harm's way as he went on. "Over a hundred, at a rough count. And eggs everywhere! I counted fifty clutches, and that was only before the patrol over the grounds chased us away."

"What news! What news!" Feniul was ecstatic. "Hundreds of hatchlings! More than fifty clutches! How wondrous!"

I cleared my throat loudly. "Excuse me, but what does this mean? Why are you so excited?"

Amacarin and Feniul both studied us, clearly shocked at our lack of enthusiasm. Finally, Feniul enlightened us.

"Have you ever seen a hatchling, Creel?"

"No." I shook my head. "I hadn't really thought about baby dragons until Niva said she had a . . . clutch." I guessed that this was the word for a group of dragon eggs.

"Precisely. Niva's clutch is the first to hatch in Feravel

in ten years." Feniul bared his teeth in some draconic emotion I couldn't fathom. "*Ten years.*"

"But why?"

"You try finding a mate when you're hiding in a cave praying the humans don't discover you," Amacarin snapped.

"Oh." I exchanged embarrassed looks with Luka and Marta. Tobin just nodded as though it made perfect sense, and one of the soldiers whispered something that sounded rather lewd to his fellow. "I'm so sorry," I told the dragons, shooting a dirty look at the soldiers.

"It's not your fault," Feniul said kindly.

"Not directly anyway," Amacarin added.

"So the dragons here don't have that problem, I guess. With finding mates." I found myself blushing, and tried not to look at Luka. He was not, nor ever would be, my mate. He was a prince, I told myself firmly. A prince.

"I believe it's more sinister than that," Amacarin said. "I think these humans are forcing them to mate, breeding them like dogs."

"I don't force my dogs to breed," Feniul protested.

"You aren't a human," Amacarin said. "You don't share humans' insistence on meddling with other creatures' lives."

Tobin gestured to his prince.

Luka nodded agreement and translated for our benefit: "We'll free Niva tonight."

"This time I'm going with you," I said firmly. "But

until it gets dark, Marta, I need you to help me make this skirt and these mirrored bits into a coat."

"A coat?" Luka looked confused at the change in topic. "Is that necessary? I thought you were too hot."

"It's not for me, it's for King Nason," I said. "Marta and I are going to be the new royal tailors."

Eggshells Underfoot

"Can you see anything?" I leaned as close to the edge as I dared, and the rock beneath my hand crumbled a little, sending sand and scree pattering down the edge of the ravine. "Oof." I drew back.

Tapping me on the shoulder, Tobin pointed to his right, and Luka and I followed him, crawling on our bellies along the edge of the ravine where the hatching grounds of the Citatian dragons were located. Feniul and Amacarin were scouting overhead, each with a soldier on his back, but there was no way for them to contact us discreetly, so we were on our own. We would have to climb down, find Niva, and, we hoped, fly her away, all before the patrol dragons caught us. With any luck, I'd be back helping Marta sew trousers for King Nason by midnight.

What Tobin had spotted was a jagged set of natural steps in the side of the cliff. Some of them were less than a hand's width, but it looked to be our best option. Again, I praised the sensibleness of the Citatian women's garb: there would be no possibility of me making the climb in skirts, even divided riding skirts. But a tunic and trousers wouldn't impede my progress.

Tobin went first, and I slithered down after him. Then he suddenly released my ankles, and I heard a dull thud.

"Tobin!" I looked over my shoulder. Luka kept coming and stepped on my hands, making me cry out briefly before I stopped myself. "Stop. Tobin fell," I whispered as loudly as I dared. Again I tried to look over my shoulder to see Tobin, but couldn't. Then I heard a scuffling sound. Feeling very daring, I leaned away from the rock wall, as much as I could, and looked straight down. Tobin was standing on a larger ledge below me, signaling frantically. I realized that he had jumped, since there were no footholds between my position and that ledge, and now he was gesturing for me to drop down to him.

Taking a deep breath, I let go of the wall. I had braced my feet for the impact on the rough ledge, but Tobin snatched me out of the air and set me down lightly beside him.

"Oh, thank you," I whispered, and moved to the side so that Luka would have room. He climbed down as far as he could and then jumped the rest of the way. Tobin put out a hand to steady him when he landed. From our now-crowded ledge, there was only a short climb down to the floor of the ravine, where our feet crunched oddly in some debris at the base of the cliff.

We all crouched down to feel what we were walking on. I recoiled as one of the sharp things sliced my index finger. Sucking on the wound, I held up the offending object to the moonlight.

"Eggshells," I breathed, pulling my finger out of my mouth.

"Dragon eggshells," Luka agreed, picking up another piece. "The place is littered with them."

Tobin made a motion, and a face.

"It's going to be cursed hard to go quietly," Luka agreed, tossing the shard aside.

We were almost tiptoeing our way across the hatching grounds, holding our breath in the hopes that we wouldn't step on a large piece of shell and give ourselves away. The grounds were filled with shallow craters holding clutches of eggs, and beside each crater was a sleeping female dragon. In the moonlight, I could only tell if they were dark or light colored. All the dragons were quite large, as though they had been carefully bred for size, something which made me feel ill. I wondered what happened to the smaller dragons, like Feniul.

Realization dawned on me and I grabbed Tobin and Luka's arms. "Niva won't have any eggs," I said. They had started to creep around the hump of a sleeping dark colored dragon to look at her face.

Tobin smacked his forehead and Luka covered his face and shook his head, embarrassed. We backed away from that dragon, and headed toward a cluster of beasts that had no eggs. I frowned at this, too. Why were they sleeping outside? Dragons needed a roof over their heads just like everyone else. To see them sleeping without the protection of a cave was one more unnatural thing in a whole slew of unnatural dragon behaviors.

My indignation was interrupted when I tripped on something that turned out to be a dragon tail the length and width of my arm. Peering down, I saw that it belonged to a hatchling. I studied the creature in wonder. It was the size of a horse, and its scales looked soft and sort of crumpled. All over its head there were round little nubs that I assumed would one day be horns. It curled its tail up tight to its body, and snuggled closer to its mother.

I crept over to another dragon. "Niva? Niva?" I called for her in a loud whisper. "Niva?"

The dragon in front of me raised her head. It wasn't Niva. Her horns were short and blunt, and I realized with horror that they had been sawed off. She was darker than Niva, and her muzzle was wider.

"Ma'am, I'm looking for my friend Niva," I said politely. "She just came here today."

With one foreclaw she plucked at the collar around her neck. She fidgeted for a moment, then sighed and laid her head back down, closing her eyes.

"Something's wrong with her," I said to Tobin, who was standing near me in a protective stance.

He tapped my arm and I looked at him. He touched his throat and mouth and then pointed around at all the dragons, shaking his head.

"The collars keep them from talking?"

He nodded.

At the sound of our whispered conversation, the dragon with the sawed-off horns opened her eyes again. At the mention of the collars, she stretched out her neck so that her head rested on the ground only a pace away from us, her eyes rolling in a piteous fashion.

Flinging my braids back over my shoulder, I stalked over to her collar in outrage. Fumbling, I tried to get the thing unbuckled but it wouldn't budge. It was too dark to see properly, but it felt like there was a strangely shaped keyhole at one side of the buckle.

"Fine," I said aloud, and pulled the knife from my belt. I was busily sawing through the leather of the collar when I heard Luka call my name softly.

As I passed Tobin I jerked a thumb back at the dragon. "Would you?"

He gave me a grim smile and pulled a foot-long dagger out of a sheath strapped to one thigh. It was serrated like a saw.

"Why didn't you show me that before?" I huffed, and went to find Luka.

Luka was on the far side of the cluster of sleeping dragons, standing by Niva. She was a little apart from the others, concealed from us by their bulk. She didn't look good. Her eyes were closed and her breathing was irregular. She looked like she'd been rolling in dust, something I knew the fastidious Niva would never do.

"Niva!" I ran to her head and stroked her muzzle, not caring if she thought me forward. "Can you hear me?"

Her eyes opened a crack and her tail twitched, but she showed no other sign of recognition.

"Let's get this collar off," I said, again wielding my small dagger with determination.

"But we don't have one of ours to replace it," Luka protested, even as he drew his own blade to help.

"I don't care," I told him. "No one's around, and Niva is strong. If we can get this one off, we can get her away from here and then deal with the pull of the slippers or whatever it is." I sawed for a while in silence, then added, "I really wish we could find out what it is they've got, and who controls the—"

I was cut off by the roar of a dragon nearby. The female with the sawed-off horns reared up on her hind legs, spreading her wings to their full extent. Blue and gold dragonfire lit the night sky and Luka and I instinctively huddled close to Niva, who still did not stir.

"By the First Fires," the newly uncollared female roared. "Krashath will pay for this!" She crouched, preparing to spring into the sky.

"Help us," I shouted at her. "Help us free our friend!"

She stopped, and her neck swiveled around to study Luka and me, crouched by Niva's head. The freed dragon reached down and with a casual swipe ripped apart Niva's collar with a claw. Then she launched herself upward without looking back.

Niva screamed as though she had been speared, writhing in the dust and broken shells of the hatching grounds. We jumped clear of her thrashing, looking around wildly as other dragons now woke. Tobin came over to the cluster of eggless females, looking concerned as Niva continued to scream and flail.

Then more dragonfire flared across the sky, and we heard roars and shouts as the Citatian night patrol encountered the dragon Tobin had freed. She bellowed at them and burned one of the patrol dragons quite badly, forcing him to land on the hatching grounds. We would soon be discovered by the patrol, or one of the awakening females would raise the alarm.

My heart in my mouth, I dove at Niva's head, wrapping my arms around it even as she tried to shake me off. "Niva! Niva! It's me, it's Creel," I shouted, no longer worrying about someone hearing us. She whipped me around so that my head snapped back, and I knew that my neck would hurt for days. But I persevered. "It's Creel, and Luka and Tobin! We're here to rescue you!"

She stopped thrashing and began to shudder—long, rattling shudders that ran from her nose to the tip of her tail. Her cries turned into a series of raw, deep dragon sobs.

"Can you hear me, Niva?" I used a more normal voice, just loud enough to be heard over her sobbing.

"Yes," she gasped out.

"Is there any . . . do you feel any power working on you? Do you need to fly somewhere? Can you feel them controlling you?"

"No," she said. "I just . . . it was so terrible."

"You don't feel any compulsion?"

"None. The collar is gone." Her shudders abated and her breathing slowed. She raised her head and looked around. "Get on my back," she said. "I want to be as far from here as possible, as fast as I can fly."

I climbed onto her back, with Luka and Tobin immediately after. Niva lurched into flight, swatting at the cluster of silent, collared females with one of her wings. It made me sick and angry to think of leaving them behind, when only a little more time and some sharper daggers could have freed them all.

"Do you think there's alchemy in each collar?" I tossed the question over my shoulder to Luka, although he hardly had any more experience with alchemy than I did. "The opposite of Milun the First's slippers?"

"I don't know," Luka shouted back. "We'll have to talk to Niva when we get to safety." His arm snaked over my shoulder to point to our right and just ahead. "Look out, Niva!"

The other freed female was in a pitched battle with the patrol. In the bursts of dragonfire, we could see that she was injured, and so were the two dragons she fought. Their fight was taking them into our path, and one of the patrol dragons had seen us.

Niva cupped her wings to stop her forward motion and then shot straight up, going high above the battle before leveling out and flying in the direction of the caves at top speed. We could no longer speak, only hold on tightly and pray to the Triune Gods.

They smiled on us, and we left the patrol dragon, which had attempted pursuit, far behind. Nevertheless, Niva made wide circles around various hills, flying low to make use of tree cover, before coming in to land at the mouth of our cave. To my great relief, Amacarin, Feniul, and Marta were there to meet us, as full of questions for Niva as we were ourselves.

But they would have to wait, for a little while. Still near hysteria, it was not until Feniul helped her to the speaking pool to contact her mate, Leontes, that she calmed down. Even after that she remained subdued, and prone to startling at the least sound. She nearly cried as she thanked us for rescuing her, which was the most unsettling thing of all.

At last Niva was ready to tell us about her ordeal.

She had been left in the net for hours, with other dragons standing watch over her. Scales were torn from her shoulder and pasted onto a blank page in a huge book. An artist sketched a portrait on the page opposite the scales—a roster of the dragons belonging to the glorious army of Citatie.

A collar was brought out, a heavy thing of leather with an iron lock the size of a human skull. The leather was doubled and sewn together with thick, scratchy thread. Bits of hair poked out of the seams and caught in Niva's neck scales. It was a most interesting discovery that our three dragon friends did not need to wear their Feravelan-made collars to resist the mind control of the Citatians. Instead, a Citatian collar only worked on the dragon it was attached to.

Once collared, it was as though she lost control of her body. She ate, slept, walked, and flew only on the command of a man named Xeran, who was assigned as her "protector," as the Citatians termed it. Her own conscious mind was still there, hovering at the back of the Citatian-controlled part of her brain, powerless to act. With deep humiliation she was forced to submit to an examination to determine if she was healthy, and then she was "put through her paces," forced to fly, flame, and lift a series of boulders to determine her speed and strength.

"In my head I was screaming," Niva confessed. "But no one could hear me."

I reached out and put one hand on her foreleg. My heart swelled with affection as Luka did the same. His face was grave.

"Madam," he said softly. "Thank you for sharing this with us. We will do everything in our power to make certain that the dragons of Citatie are freed even as you were."

I reached out and put my other hand in Luka's and gave it a squeeze.

Making a Scene

G ood day to you, Captain," I said to the man barring our way. "We're here to see the king."

Dressed in the white tunic and breeches of the Citatian army, and topped with the requisite spiked helmet, the guardsman gleamed in the sun. He squinted down at us in disbelief, visibly turning over my words in his head, searching for a translation that would make sense.

Marta and I, clad in our finest Citatian trousers and tunics, thin beaded slippers, and brilliant sashes, stood on the scorching pavement and smiled. I had dyed two of my braids blue, and Marta had rubbed beeswax on hers so that they wouldn't appear so frayed.

At our feet rested a basket containing our handiwork: a suit of clothes made of embroidered Feravelan satin and trimmed with mirrored silk. Luka had given us the king's dimensions as best he could, judging the man to be slightly less than his own height, narrower in the shoulder but thicker in the middle, and we had worked with that.

"You want . . . to see . . . King Nason?" The soldier's

question was labored, both from an uneasy command of Feravelan and apparent disbelief at our request. He studied our clothes and the basket. "What . . . business?"

From what we'd heard of Nason, if you weren't invited to the palace, you could spend months waiting for an audience. Luka, who had been an expected royal ambassador, had still waited on the king's pleasure for six days. He had met a man wandering the corridors who said he had been living in an empty antechamber for nine months, trying to gain an audience to settle a land dispute. The man was haggard and his finery in tatters, but he knew that if he stayed nearby, Nason would eventually summon him.

I wondered if he was still here.

"We are the finest tailors in the world," I said, opening my arms wide. "We are here to present his Effulgence with a new suit of clothes." I threw open the lid of the basket and showed the guard captain the scarlet and gold coat folded on top. He reached out to touch it with one dirty finger, and Marta slapped his hand away.

"No, no," she scolded. "This is for the king."

Growing red, the man glared at her. "I must look for . . . danger. Weapons."

"Good man," I said. I leaned down and, as delicately as if I were lifting a baby, drew the coat from the basket. Marta picked up the tunic and trousers with equal care, and we wafted them up and down to show that there were no concealed weapons or tiny assassins waiting to leap out at the king. The guard looked into the empty basket suspiciously and then at the shining fabric we held.

"Very well." An ugly grin split his face. "The king will . . . maybe . . . see you. This year."

While we refolded the clothing he stepped back and gave the order for the gates to be opened. Marta and I went past him with our heads high, the basket carried between us. I gave the man a courteous nod, as though he had been gracious.

"Well, we made it past the first obstacle," Marta said out of the corner of her mouth as we went across the courtyard.

Then we had no more breath to spare. The front doors of the Crown Palace were at the top of a mountain of stairs made from gleaming white stone. It was nearly noon, and the heat beat down on us as we trudged up the stairs, holding the basket between us and feeling the baking-hot marble burn our feet through the soles of our light slippers.

"I still think that Nason wants Feravel because Citatie is too hot," Marta panted.

"And full of monkeys," I added.

She shot me a dark look. "He's still learning."

"He'd better learn fast, or Amacarin might eat him."

Marta had named her monkey Ruli, and even as we spoke Ruli was probably tearing apart our cave. He screamed constantly, shredded any parchment he could get his little hands on, and urinated on anyone who offended him.

And he was very easy to offend.

Grimacing as we reached the top of the stairs, I said in a low voice, "We may have to uncollar each dragon by hand."

"But first, the king," Marta said.

Judging by the rumpled clothes and disarranged coiffures of the others waiting to see Nason, some of them had slept there at least one night. I gave Marta a despairing look. She tossed her braids over her shoulder and marched to the wide doors at the opposite end of the room, dragging me and the basket along with her.

"We're here to see his Effulgence," Marta told the guards at the doors. Her voice was bright, confident, and she showed not the slightest bit of notice for the outraged stares of the other people waiting. "Laan no tishbaln verr Nason-e," she said, repeating our goal in Citatian. Luka had coached us in a few phrases, but assured us that the king spoke Feravelan as well.

The guard pointed to some chairs. "You wait," he said, smirking. "Wait long time maybe."

"No," I said loudly.

"Have to," he said, smirking even more gleefully. "Wait, wait, wait."

Marta drew a deep breath. "We have to wait?" Her voice rose an octave on the last word. Lower lip trembling, tears welled in her big blue eyes.

Stifling my admiration, I stepped into the fray.
"You've made her cry," I snapped at the guard, patting
Marta's back. "You awful man! And imagine what the
king will say when he finds out that you kept us waiting
here . . . kept *him* waiting for us to bring his new
clothes!" I swept an arm around the room. "We
shouldn't be here at all! Look at these people! Peasants
with land disputes! Common merchants! Gah!"

The flood of words gave the guard pause, then his
brow cleared and he gave me an appalled look. "King . . .
wait? King . . . ask for . . . clothes?" He pointed at the
basket.

I whipped back the lid to show him the satin coat,
while Marta continued to blubber in fine style. "Yes," I
said, pointing to the embroidery of the coat. "The king's
new coat," I said loudly and clearly, as though speaking
to an idiot. Then I put the lid back on and patted Marta's
arm this time. "Don't worry," I soothed, still in a voice
that carried. "We'll tell the king this man wouldn't let us
see him."

A moment later we were ushered through the door
and down a short corridor. We found ourselves standing
before another pair of guards, very large men holding
unsheathed scimitars. The doors that they guarded were
plated with gold and inlaid with lapis lazuli and onyx.

"We have brought the king's clothing, as requested,"
I said boldly, before Marta had to start crying again.

The guards were so alike that I thought they must be

brothers, if not twins, and now they raised their eyebrows in perfect synchronicity. They looked at us, then at each other, then at the basket. Once more, I pulled off the lid to reveal the contents.

At last they stepped aside to let us pass through the golden doors and we were ushered into the presence of King Nason of Citatie.

White As Bone

No stranger to courts and kings, and wanting to keep up my brash pose, I took several steps into the throne room before I noticed the silence and the emptiness. I drew up short, looking around the cavernous room with its dim lamps reflecting off marble pillars and gilded chairs that no one was sitting on.

Then Marta made a small noise and let go of her end of the basket, and I saw the dragon.

Curled at the far end of the room, just behind the throne of hammered gold, was one of the largest dragons I had ever seen. His body was easily as big as a good-sized cottage, and his neck and tail made him even longer and more imposing. It was hard to tell, because he was coiled up, but I thought he might be as large as Shardas, who was the biggest dragon in Feravel.

This dragon, however, was as white as bone.

It opened its eyes, which were black and flat like a snake's, and looked at us. Marta made that noise again, and I dropped my end of the basket, unnerved by the cold malice of the dragon's gaze.

"Mehel? Mehel rioho?" A shrill voice cut the air and a figure climbed out of the coils of the dragon's tail.

It was a man, roughly thirty years old, and wearing fine, brightly colored silks. On his head was an ornamental silver helmet with three enormous plumes on top; a large gold sunburst set with an egg-sized ruby adorned the front. The helmet was slightly askew, showing curly white-blond hair that reminded me of a sheep's fleece.

"You're not Citatian? Are you Roulaini? You're not Feravelan, are you? Why did you wake me?" He rubbed his eyes and then straightened his helmet. He straightened his whole body, in fact, quite suddenly. His expression changed from confusion to disdain and he glared at us instead of blinking sleepily. "What is your business here?"

I curtsied deeply, which felt odd in the trousers I was wearing. "We're here to fit your new suit, Your Majesty," I said in Citatian. It was another of the useful phrases that Luka had taught me.

"Oh." He frowned. "I don't recall ordering a new suit, and certainly not from *Feravelan* tailors." To my relief he spoke in Feravelan. I was reaching the limit of my Citatian vocabulary.

Giving a sigh of false regret, I bowed my head and Marta did the same. "Your Majesty is too clever by half," I said mournfully. "We had hoped that your Effulgence would be so caught up in affairs of state that you would not see through our ruse. We humbly wish to be your royal tailors, Your Majesty, and so we have snuck into the palace that we might present this gift to you."

With a flourish we took the lid off the basket and lifted out the suit of clothing. I held the coat with real pride: I had cut up my favorite riding dress to make it. It was scarlet satin, embroidered with a pattern of gold and orange and blue flames. I had added lapels and cuffs of the mirrored silk in bands of color to complement the embroidery. The shirt and trousers were of straw yellow and blue, respectively, and the seams were stitched with scarlet thread for contrast.

"It's so gaudy," the king said in an uncertain tone. "And what's this pattern?" He fingered the flame design on the coat.

"Dragonfire," I said, almost feeling jealous as he touched it. I hadn't had a chance to wear this riding dress myself before hacking it to pieces to give to Nason. I'd been waiting for a good opportunity to show it off in front of Shardas . . . and maybe Luka.

"A ruler of Your Majesty's great presence should step forth, bold and proud, in all the colors of the rainbow, sire," Marta said, when I failed to elaborate.

I raised my eyebrows at this, trying not to let out a slightly hysterical giggle. We had used this same pitch on a very large and forceful dowager duchess not too many weeks ago. The woman had a dozen grandchildren and was shaped like the prow of a ship, yet persisted in wearing demure, girlish pastels. This argument had convinced her to purchase a gown of plum satin more flattering than anything she had worn in at least twenty years.

My heart in my throat, I held the coat out at shoulder height. "May I, Your Majesty?" I had expected to be thrown out long before now.

The dragon behind the throne hissed, and his tail flexed and coiled with a dry sound. The black eyes had never left us, but now they seemed more fixed. It had a collar, a wide band of gold and jewels, but for the first time I felt no pity, no outrage. I was glad this dragon was collared and under control. Even so, it seemed dangerous.

"Please try on the coat, sire," Marta wheedled. "It must be properly tailored for the full glorious effect."

The king hesitated a moment more. "The guards searched you for weapons?"

"Indeed they did, sire," I assured him.

"Very well."

He held out his arms and we took off the yellow silk coat he wore, replacing it with the one we had made. The sleeves were a bit long, which would be difficult to fix, because of the cuffs, and the shoulders were too wide. Really, Marta or I could have stood in as a tailor's dummy; the king was hardly an inch taller than she and nearly as slender as I. With a bit of chalk from the pouch at my waist I made marks on the coat. Next, we held up the trousers and tunic to judge their fit.

"It wouldn't be seemly for us to watch you try them on," Marta said.

"I insist," King Nason protested, and promptly unfastened his trousers.

Naturally it was at that moment that the rest of his court entered the room. Later we learned that the courtiers always left the king alone to eat lunch and have a brief rest, which is why he was unattended when we arrived. But the period of royal solitude concluded for the day just as the king's trousers fell around his ankles and some three dozen people filed in via small side doors, to see Marta and me standing red-faced in front of a bare-legged king.

A man in a purple hat with a golden sunburst brooch affixed to the front stepped forward, an expression of distaste on his face. He started to make shooing gestures at us, saying something in Citatian that I have no doubt was unflattering.

"No, no," I said, shaking my head. "We're the tailors. Tailors!" I held out the trousers to the king, averting my face from his state of undress. Ignoring the other man, ignoring the entire court, really, the king took them from me and slipped them on.

Citatian trousers fit loosely, which meant that we wouldn't have to make any adjustments. Not only did we not have any experience in fitting trousers, I didn't relish the thought of having to mark and pin the king's trousers with him in them.

The purple-hatted man said something to the king, who replied airily in kind. Whatever he said mollified the man somewhat, and he turned to us with a less shocked expression.

"Tailors?"

"Yes, sir," we piped in unison.

"*Feravelan* tailors?" He studied us coldly.

"Yes, sir," I said, an expression of deep innocence on my face. "We are people of no importance in any land, and would not dream of causing trouble."

"Very well." His voice was dismissive. "See that you don't. We have no quarrel with Feravel's *tailors*, in any case."

I opened my mouth to ask who they did have a quarrel with, but Marta elbowed me in the ribs.

"I am the grand vizier," the man told us. "Lord Arjas."

We curtsied and introduced ourselves, and turned back to the king to find him struggling to pull his tunic over his helmet. He was quite stuck, and revealing a great deal of pasty, narrow chest to his court. Marta and I rushed to help, along with Lord Arjas.

"He should have taken off the helmet," I said as we extracted the king. Glancing around, I saw that the court appeared not the least bit startled or discomfited by the development, and wondered what a typical day was like in the throne room.

"I never take it off," the king said with dignity as his head popped free. "Never, ever." He straightened the helmet with great seriousness. "A king does not bare his head before his underlings."

"Forgive us, Your Majesty," Marta said.

Picking up our shirt, I looked helplessly from the neck hole to the king's headgear. Even with the laces at the neck completely undone, I worried that the sharp steel spike would catch the fabric and rip it.

Seeing my dilemma, the grand vizier took the shirt from me and studied it. "This will not fit, Your Majesty," he said.

"Then fix it. You *are* tailors, after all," Nason said to us.

"But your helmet might tear it, sire," I said.

"His Majesty will have to try it on later, in private," Lord Arjas said.

"But I want it now," the king protested, and then quite suddenly he yanked off the helmet and tossed it to me. I barely managed to catch it.

"Quickly," the king ordered Marta, who hurried to drop the shirt over his head.

Lord Arjas looked alarmed, and I stepped forward so that I could replace the helmet as soon as the king's head poked through the neck of the shirt. As I did, I glanced down at the interior of the helmet and froze.

Arjas snatched it from my hands and clapped it back onto the king's head. He helped Marta lace up the shirt, and Marta measured and pinned it alone as I stood and watched.

It was Marta, too, who made the arrangements for us to bring the clothing back the day after tomorrow, and

Marta who repacked the basket and led me from the throne room.

Back in the cave, with Luka and Tobin demanding to know what had happened, I found my voice again.

"Marta, did you see that?"

"See what?" Luka was practically dancing from foot to foot with impatience. "What did you see?"

"The king's helmet is lined with dragon scales," Marta answered for me. "White ones, like that horrible dragon he has in his throne room." She shuddered.

"You didn't tell us there was a dragon in the throne room," I choked out.

Luka looked abashed and put an arm around me. I pressed against him, not caring if the soldiers were watching. "I, er, didn't want to worry you. It's so weird and horrible, that white dragon. And I know how you feel about collaring dragons, so I didn't want to upset you by telling you that the king keeps one as a pet in his throne room."

I pulled away from him. *"You didn't want to upset me?!"* I lowered my voice, forcing myself to concentrate on the matter at hand, rather than argue with Luka about things I did and didn't need to be protected from. "Don't you understand?" I felt nauseated, and found myself leaning against Feniul for support. "I think their method is reversed: to control a dragon, you put a collar on it with some of your hair or blood worked into it rather than having one alchemical object that controls them all."

"Yes, Niva told us that." Luka still looked puzzled.

"But the king's helmet is made from dragon scales," I said again. "And he never takes it off for longer than a few seconds."

Niva, however, was not puzzled. She lumbered to her feet and rattled her wings, drawing all eyes to her. "You can't mean?"

"I do mean," I replied. My knees were shaking, and I sank down on the nearest cot. "The other Citatian dragons may be under human control, but that white dragon is controlling the king."

A Plume of Steam

The clamor in the cave was deafening. There was no doubting what we had seen. Marta and I agreed that the white dragon had given us chills long before I saw what could only have been a helmet of scales on King Nason's head. And I would never forget how the king's expression had changed from slack-jawed stupor to alert wariness in the blink of an eye when the helmet came off. But now there was the question of what to do.

Luka wanted to contact his father as speedily as possible and Niva wanted to notify Shardas. I gave her a look when she said his name in front of the soldiers, but she just snorted.

"It is too late for such secrecy," she said tartly. "If the human king is to be told, the dragon king surely must be."

"You have a king?" One of the soldiers looked amazed, and I realized that knowing Shardas was alive when only a moment before they hadn't known he existed, didn't make them much of a threat to his safety.

Snapping my fingers, I nodded at Niva. "Yes, tell

Shardas everything, and ask if he will send your mate to King Caxel. He could be in the King's Seat in a matter of hours, rather than days." Luka had been on the verge of sending one of the soldiers with us to deliver the message, a journey of at least three weeks if he rode nonstop and took the fastest ship he could find. Niva went out to the pool to deliver the message.

"And in the meantime what do we do?" Luka began to pace. "The dragons are controlled by soldiers who get their orders from the king—"

"Who is, in turn, controlled by a dragon," I said, finishing his sentence. "But why? Why would a dragon want to start a war against humans?"

"And Feravel in particular?" Marta added. "Remember, the war is aimed at Feravel; Roulain just happens to be in the way."

"What does it *want?*" Luka looked frustrated, as we all did.

Tobin gestured, and Marta translated for the soldiers' benefit. "Feravel's relations with Citatie have always been good. Perhaps it is the white dragon we need to deal with."

I nodded. "We have to find out if the dragon is behind it all, and if it isn't, then who is? It's not King Nason, that's for sure."

"Do we tell people?" Luka asked. "But who? And who would believe us? After all: we're Feravelan."

"We could tell the grand vizier," I suggested. "He seemed like a sensible man."

"But how do we get him alone?" Marta pointed out. "When we bring the king his suit we'll be in a room full of people, and that horrible dragon will suspect something if we ask to speak to Lord Arjas alone." She shivered and Tobin put his arm around her.

"Perhaps if I requested an audience with Arjas," Luka mused.

Tobin interrupted, signing to the prince one-handed, the other hand still rubbing Marta's shoulder. "How do you get an audience when you've been sentenced to death?" Marta interpreted.

I spoke up. "I want to find that dragon, the one I . . . well, Tobin . . . uncollared. Perhaps she knows how long this has been going on, and what the white dragon is up to."

One of the soldiers, a man named Junn, spoke up. "I think that lady dragon has been getting up to some more mischief," he said.

"How so?" Luka ran his hands through his short hair as he listened, making it stand on end. He looked even younger when he did it, and I realized with a start that he was barely eighteen and trying to stop a war. Again.

I took up Nason's new coat and began to alter it while we talked. As my silly aunt used to say, idleness knits the garters of devilry.

"Well, I flew out on that fellow Feniul this morning, as ordered," Junn told us. "And we saw some excitement over by them dragon hatching grounds. Feniul flew in close as he dared, and we saw half a dozen dragons patrolling the area. He said they were talking about 'five more being gone, with their hatchlings.' I guessed that meant that five more of them females had gone haring off. And who would take those collars off, but that lady dragon you all set free?"

"Good for her!" I held my needle in my mouth while I applauded and then spit it back into my palm to keep sewing. "So there're at least six free now?"

"The message is on its way to the human king of Feravel," Niva said, coming into the cave. "And Creel, Shardas would like to speak to you."

I put down my sewing and followed her back out. Once I reached the pool, Niva stepped away to give us some privacy. I sat on a low rock at the edge and leaned over to see my friend.

Shardas looked better, even in the week or so since I had last seen him. The scales around his face were almost completely new, and his sapphire horns were sharp and bright. His blue eyes were dark with rage, however, and I drew back, wondering if it was me he was angry with.

"Creel? Are you all right?" His deep voice was tight with concern.

"Yes, I'm fine," I said hesitantly. "How are you?"

"I? I am appalled that I sent you there to face this with only *Feniul* to protect you," he snarled.

"Feniul is all right," I protested. Usually Shardas was fondly exasperated by his cousin; I had never heard him insult the green dragon before. "And I have Niva and Amacarin; there's no direct danger."

"*No direct danger!*" A plume of steam actually shot out of the pool, narrowly missing me. "Krashath! *Krashath* is controlling the king of Citatie!"

I leaned as far forward as I dared. "You know the white dragon?"

"There is no such thing as a white dragon," Shardas said, and his voice was like the scraping of swords. "He was once the color of polished silver, until he delved so deeply into alchemy that he bleached his scales white! *Krashath!*" His loathing was so strong that I thought the water between us would curdle like old milk. "I thought he was dead."

"How? Why?" I wasn't sure which question to ask, or what sort of answer I was looking for. I had never seen Shardas like this, not even when he had told me about Milun the First, who had betrayed Velika. He was practically vibrating with rage.

"I did my best to kill him, but it seems my best was not good enough," Shardas continued, oblivious to my questions. "And now he is planning this . . . this! He will destroy us all, to get what he wants."

"What does he want?" I felt a spark of hope. "Is there something we can give him? A rare book? Jewels?"

"*No!*" More steam came out of the pool. "What he wants . . . he cannot have. Never. He must be destroyed."

"All right." I had to scoot back even farther to avoid being burned by the steam. "But how?"

He shook his head. "Do nothing, *nothing* until I get there."

"What?" Now I shook mine. "But Shardas, you can't!"

"I can and I will."

The image rippled, and the pool was just a pool again. I stirred the heated water frantically with my fingers, but could not summon Shardas again. I hurried into the cave, nearly tripping over Amacarin's tail in my haste.

"We have to stop him," I pleaded, going to Niva. "Shardas says he is coming here. He says that this white dragon is named Krashath, and that he must destroyed. And Shardas will come here, but he can't! His wings! His scales! He's too weak!" There were tears on my cheeks and I tugged at Niva's foreleg as though she could get up and do something to stop Shardas right that moment.

"Krashath?! Is he certain?" Niva's nostrils flared, and Luka ducked in case she lost control of her fire. "By the First Fires," Niva breathed. "This is unwelcome news."

"To say the least," Amacarin snapped. "Krashath still alive? It's a nightmare!"

"Who is Krashath?" Feniul looked confused. And also annoyed, as Marta's monkey was sitting on his muzzle and reaching into one of his nostrils with both tiny fists.

"You are what? Three hundred years old?"

Feniul nodded. "Three hundred and twelve."

"It was before your hatching, then," Niva explained. "But only by three decades or so. Krashath wanted to be king, but he was very unpopular. His fondness for alchemy was worrying, and he had a rather cavalier attitude toward his fellow dragons. He felt no qualms about ordering his fellows about, having younger or less intelligent dragons clean his lair or bring him food, and he also put forth the idea of hiring out dragons as mercenaries for human armies."

"And he's still pursuing that," I said slowly. "Using alchemy to force other dragons to fight."

"Shardas defeated him," Niva continued. "We all thought that Krashath died of his wounds, but it seems not."

"So that's how you become king of the dragons?" Luka's eyes were wide. "You fight your rival to the death?"

"Not usually, no," Niva said, shaking her head. "Once the queen has chosen her mate, there is usually little argument. But Velika was young, and Krashath seemed convinced that she would change her mind if she saw that he was more powerful than his . . . rival."

She started to say something else, but I held up my hands. "Wait, wait! So, Shardas is the king because Velika chose him?"

"That's right."

"How did she become queen?"

Niva assumed an expression that meant she was about to tell me something about dragons that I should already have known. I gritted my teeth: I disliked feeling ignorant, especially when I was trying to stop a war.

"Velika Azure-Wing is descended from the First Dragon, the mother of all dragons, who exploded out of the First Fires twelve thousand years ago. The queenship has been passed down from mother to daughter, directly, from that time."

Luka cocked his head to one side. "Then why is it that everyone takes orders from Shardas? Shouldn't Velika be in command?"

"Our queens are, you might say, the spiritual rulers among us. When the queen is strong, dragons prosper. We go to her when there is illness or injury, she blesses us when we mate, and sings the mourning song when we die. The king takes command when there is danger: wars, rogues like Krashath, mountains erupting, earthshakes, and the like. Sadly, in recent centuries, there has been more need for the king than the queen."

"And the queen was lost," I pointed out, and then felt tactless for reminding them. Then something occurred to me.

"Did Krashath depose the king of the Citatian dragons, then? And what about their queen?" I swallowed. "You don't think he collared them, do you?"

Amacarin shook his head and rolled his eyes, as

though in despair of my ignorance, before leaning in close to me. "We who can fly see no need to be constrained by you humans' physical borders," he said. "We have one king and one queen."

My mouth opened in an "O." "Shardas is the king of all the dragons in the world? And Velika is the queen? Of the world?" I was agog at this information. How could Velika and Shardas have done so much? How could the dragons have survived so long without a queen?

I must have said this last thought aloud because Amacarin lashed his tail. "It has . . . not been easy. Shardas took Velika's loss very hard, and in many lands we went into hiding. But we are an independent race." He shrugged.

Niva dipped her head at me. "What were Shardas's instructions?"

"Er, we're to be careful, and not call any attention to ourselves until he gets here," I said, swallowing and thinking of my earlier fears. "But *can* he get here? His wings!" My voice choked on the last word; as I imagined Shardas falling from the sky, his tattered wings unable to bear his weight.

"He knows his own strengths," Niva reassured me. "Even in this matter I do not think he would be hotheaded enough to commit folly. We must do as he says."

"All right," Luka said uneasily. "And we'll see what my father can do as well."

"Very good." Niva inclined her head graciously.

"There's just one little problem," Marta said, looking wary of bringing it up.

"What is that?" Niva eyed her.

"Creel and I have to return to the palace the day after tomorrow to deliver these clothes to the king." She sucked in her breath. "And Krashath will be there."

Under Krashath's Scrutiny

After discovering that the king of Citatie was controlled by a dragon, and then further learning that said dragon was evil, I planned never to see the king or his dragon again.

I was here to help—to save my country and her people (and dragons). But I knew my limitations, and defeating an evil dragon single-handedly was definitely beyond my power. Furthermore, I had promised Shardas that I would stay clear of Krashath, which had seemed an easy enough promise to keep at the time.

But then Luka and I went to the Grand Market the next day to buy the almond pastries we had all come to love. It was awkward, the two of us walking around, trying to pretend that we were just friends. The truth was, I wished with all my heart that we could be more, but in turning down Miles, I felt that I had shut the door on any alliance with the royal family. King Caxel certainly seemed to think so. If only he hadn't offered me the wrong prince! Luka and I might already be married, instead of swallowing our feelings in the face of his father's wrath.

A basket of the steaming pastries over my arm, I heard a chattering noise and turned to see my old friend the monkey seller waving at me, another little black-and-white ball of trouble clinging to his sleeve.

"Hello, hello, maidy!" He waved the monkey under my nose, and I quickly sidestepped. Marta's horrible little Ruli had cured me of any desire I might have ever had to own one of my own. "Monkey?" He thrust the creature at me again.

"No! No monkeys," I said, holding out my hands in a defensive gesture. I pasted on a smile, though, so that he wouldn't take offense.

"Monkey, youngsir?" He brandished the creature at Luka.

Having had his best shirt shredded by Ruli that morning, Luka had no trouble refusing. "No, I thank you. It's too cold in Feravel for monkeys."

The monkey seller's face clouded. "No, no! Pretty maidy, youngsir, not go back! Feravel bad. All burn soon."

"How soon?" Luka and I said at the same time.

The man's dark eyes rolled to the sky, where dragons carrying white-uniformed soldiers wheeled in training formations. "Soon," he said in a whisper. "You stay Pelletie, nice maidy, nice youngsir. Feravel all gone soon."

"When?" Luka hunched down to the smaller man's level, ignoring the monkey as it delightedly plucked at the laces of his tunic sleeve. "Next month? Next week?"

The man pursed his lips, making a face like a new baby about to cry. "Brother sell sheep to army for feed dragons. He say one day, two days. Brother sell all sheep today, dragons eat all, get ready for long flight."

"In two days?" My voice rose, and I clamped my mouth shut before we called attention to ourselves.

"Sh-sh-sh!" The monkey seller put a thin brown finger to my lips and I fought the urge to flinch away. "Two days. Bad for Feravel. You hide, maybe?"

"Yes, yes, thank you." Luka gave the man a coin, grabbed my arm, and steered me away. "Let's get some bread and meat, and get back to the cave," he said in my ear.

We quickly finished our shopping and almost ran out of the city gates to the small hill and juniper grove that hid Feniul. We shouted the news to him as he flew us back to our cave, and then we told the others.

"We have to stall Krashath," Niva said when she heard. "We have to prevent his army from flying north."

"How?" Amacarin's tail lashed, and he knocked several of the cots over.

"We need to talk to the grand vizier," I said, righting a cot and recovering my sewing, which had been scattered in the upset. "Krashath doesn't want people to know that he's controlling the king. If we can convince the grand vizier of what's going on, I'm certain that he can buy us some time."

"If we uncollared more of the dragons," Niva mused, "they could help us fight."

"If we told the vizier," I pointed out, "he might be able to order the dragons uncollared."

"We just have to make certain that everyone is careful," Luka said. "We don't know what Krashath will do if his plot is exposed."

"Oh, dear," Marta sighed. "It looks like Creel and I are headed back to the palace to fit the king's new coat."

"I'm afraid so," Luka agreed.

"At least the pay is usually good, sewing for royalty," I said philosophically. Everyone stared at me. "It was a *joke*," I protested.

"Humans have no real sense of humor," Amacarin said with a sniff.

Since none of us had ever heard Amacarin attempt anything like a joke, we kept silent.

The next day Marta and I presented ourselves at the gates of the palace once more. This time, however, we were ushered straight into the throne room, with no need for tears or deception. The entire court was present, including the grand vizier, and, of course, Krashath.

I did my best to ignore the white dragon. The mind-numbed Citatian dragons were generally ignored, and it would ruin everything if we were to reveal that we knew Krashath was more than a status symbol for the king.

So, keeping my eyes firmly on the king and away from Krashath, I checked the fit of Nason's new coat. All the while, I tried to draw the attention of the grand vizier, to see if we couldn't catch him alone or arrange to speak with him privately.

When I finally caught his eye, he came over to admire Nason's new suit. I sidled over to Lord Arjas and waited until other courtiers joined us to praise our work. While Marta entertained them, I tapped the vizier's elbow and murmured my request for a private audience.

"Why?" He looked frankly startled and his voice was a good deal louder than I would have liked.

"Um, well, I need to talk to you about . . . gaining citizenship. Of Citatie. Marta and I both," I hedged. I had thought from the vizier's worried looks the other day that he knew something was amiss, and perhaps he did, but it seemed that he was not expecting help from uppity female Feravelan tailors.

"Do you not have the proper permit to work here?" He looked scandalized.

I summoned my most winning smile. "Of course we do!" I made a mental note to see if Luka or one of the soldiers couldn't forge one for us. "But it's so hard to find a permanent place to live and work when one is a foreigner. We thought it might be easier if we were citizens."

"I see." But his brow was wrinkled in consternation. "Come to my study tomorrow, the both of you, just after third bell, and we can speak about it."

"Thank you." My smile became even more genuine.

"You haven't petted my dragon," King Nason

announced, pushing through the crowd of courtiers admiring his new coat. He grabbed my arm with one hand and Marta's elbow with the other. She shot me a panicked look as the king marched us up the length of the throne room toward the coiled white form of Krashath. "Isn't he magnificent?! The only white dragon ever hatched!" Nason let go of my arm to slap Krashath's flank in a proprietary way.

A sharp flick of the dragon's tail was the only sign that the white beast even felt Nason's hand on him. I had expected something to show in his eyes at this cavalier treatment: a glimpse of disgust, of anger, but there was nothing, only two dead black pools that seemed to . . .

"Creel?" Marta's hand on my arm drew me back to the present.

"Very nice, Your Majesty," I said, trying to keep my voice from trembling.

"Pet him," Nason ordered.

I felt my gorge rise as I reached out a tentative hand. Krashath shifted a little, obligingly moving closer to me. It struck me that he wasn't disgusted at this condescending behavior: he was forcing the king to ask this of me. Krashath *wanted* me to touch him, and his reasons could not be good.

May the Triunity forever bless her; Marta came to my rescue and made another scene.

Just as my hand, flesh crawling, was about to touch Krashath's flank, Marta announced to the room in general that she was feeling far too warm, and rather dizzy besides. I withdrew my hand and turned to look at her with feigned concern. She reeled toward me, one hand to her brow.

"Oh, help, Creel," she cried out, and then fainted into my arms.

If I hadn't seen her do this over a dozen times, I would have been quite worried for her. Her performance was very convincing, and the rest of the room was clearly taken in, rushing to offer cool drinks and a couch for her to rest on. But since she was justly proud of her skill and had tried to teach "theatrical fainting" to me and our friend Alle on a number of occasions, I was mostly grateful for the interruption.

Trying to look anxious, I carried her to the proffered couch and laid her on it. While I fanned her and someone applied a dampened handkerchief to her forehead, I explained to Nason and Arjas that Marta was very sensitive to the heat.

"They are lying."

There was no mistaking who had said this. Dragon voices sound like rocks being scraped together, and Krashath's was particularly loud and harsh. The twittering over Marta's faint died instantly, and one of the ladies of the court fainted in earnest.

"It talks," gasped a large woman, her face rigid with shock.

"How astonishing!" Lord Arjas threw up his hands

in a startled gesture that I thought looked a little forced. I frowned at him, but didn't have the time to study him too closely.

"Yes, yes, of course! If he senses danger," Nason said, his words tumbling over each other. "Guards, seize them!" He pointed a finger at me and Marta.

Recognizing that our ploy had failed, Marta sat up, causing the court to glare and murmur accusingly. She gave them a defiant look. Meanwhile, I decided to lay it all out on the table, as the guards stalked toward us with bared scimitars.

"Lord Arjas, Krashath is controlling the king, not the other way 'round," I said, reaching out a hand to him and trying to sound as sincere as I could. "You have to believe us: the king's helmet allows the dragon to control him. Krashath was supposed to be dead for his crimes in Feravel—you must believe me!"

But Arjas's face was closed and still. He stepped aside without a word as the guards came forward. One grabbed me by the arm, the other seized Marta, and they forced us to our knees in front of Nason.

"Clear the room," Nason ordered, and his shocked courtiers filed out. Even the guards let go of our shoulders and stiffly exited the room.

"Your outburst is going to cause a great deal of trouble, young woman," Arjas said once the doors had been closed. He frowned at me.

"Let Marta go," I told Arjas. The king's face was

completely blank, and I knew he would be deaf to any pleas. "I'll tell you anything you need to know. But first you have to believe me: Krashath is controlling the king."

Arjas laughed. "I knew that already." He shook his head with mock regret. "But the court didn't, and that's why your little scene was so troublesome. I can't very well have the entire court executed to stop the rumors."

He said this last as if it were an option he might still consider. I suppressed a shudder even as my mind turned over what he had said.

"You knew?" Marta gasped.

"Of course! Krashath and I have been working for this for over a year. He came to me with his army of dragons, and I gave him access to this idiot." Arjas's lips twisted in distaste as he indicated the king. "It was ridiculously easy to put that scale-lined helmet on him. The difficult part was convincing the generals that coherent orders for the invasion of Feravel had actually come from our mad king."

Marta and I could only stand and gape. Arjas, the Grand Vizier of Citatie, had helped a dragon take control of his king's mind. We had talked of him as though he were a potential ally, but he was just as much an enemy as Krashath himself.

"You smell of *him*," Krashath said suddenly.

A light kindled in his black eyes, and he crept across the floor toward us. I took a step back, and his tail whipped around behind me, keeping me from running.

"You smell of my hated brother."

I went cold all over. The thin silk tunic I wore had once been a shift, but I had cut it off at the knees and hemmed it to the Citatian style just the day before. The last time I had worn it, I had been at the cave with Shardas and Velika, and there had not been time to launder it since then. Krashath's nose was over a pace long: he could smell things that a dog could only hope to sniff out.

"Shardas is your brother?" The words popped out before I could stop them.

"You know my brother well?" The tip of Krashath's nose was only a handspan from my chest as he sniffed at my tunic. One large black eye studied me, his head atilt. "You know him very well." It was no longer a question.

"He is coming to kill you," Marta said, defiant. "He knows you're here, and he's coming for you."

"Is he?" Krashath's tongue flicked out and his eyes half closed. "Is he now? How delightful."

"You won't think that," I chimed in, since there was no point in hiding it now, "when he's blasting you and Arjas into ash." Despite my words there was a cold, sour twist in my stomach.

"We shall see who becomes ash, human," Krashath said. "I am more than ready to face my brother." He reared back a little, and his tongue flicked out again. "In fact, why don't you call to him? Tell him to hurry to my city." He reached out and grasped Marta with one foreclaw and me with the other. "Tell him to hurry before you fall."

And with that, Krashath hurtled out the long windows of the throne room. Shards of glass scratched my face and caught in my hair as we broke out into the air above the courtyard. Krashath hovered there only a moment, while below us there were screams and the sound of horses panicking. Then he shot upward, up among the towers of the palace. Without warning he opened his claws and dropped us on the conical copper roof of one of the highest towers, then flew away, laughing.

Letting Go

"Creel! Are you all right?"

I thought this was very sweet of Marta to ask, considering that she, too, was clinging to the spike that rose from the pinnacle of the roof. Her eyes were squeezed shut, and she was scrabbling at the smooth copper surface with her slippered feet.

My position was little better. I had my hands just above Marta's, and my legs sprawled wide, stretching them around the conical roof as much as I could. It was not unlike riding a very large dragon. A very large dragon that was flying straight up with little concern for its passenger's safety. Still, if I didn't find a more secure position soon, my arms would be pulled out of their sockets by the weight of my body.

Blood pounding in my ears, I dared to look down the slope of the roof. I concentrated very hard on looking only at the edge of the roof, and not beyond it at the open space through which I could fall endlessly before splattering onto a lower roof or even the courtyard all the way below. . . .

Dragging my attention back to the roof, I saw that the edge jutted out, creating a ledge some two handspans wide. It wasn't much, but if we lay against the roof and stood on the ledge, we could stay up here much longer than if we had to hold ourselves up with the spike.

"Marta, there's a little lip on the edge of the roof. We're going to have to slide down and stand there. If we try to hold on here, we'll get hand cramps and fall."

"I'm not sliding down this roof, Creel." Her words were perfectly rational, but there was a hysterical edge to her voice. "We'll keep sliding, right off that little lip. . . ." She trailed off into a moan as she looked past the ledge.

I realized that she was right. The copper roof was very slick, and twice as high as we were tall. By the time we hit the ledge we would have gathered enough speed that we would be lucky if we didn't go flying right off the meager foothold and into open air.

"Think, Creel, think," I muttered.

"Ooh, I looked again," Marta said. "I think I might be sick."

"Don't! You'll make the roof even slicker," I told her. "It's bad enough that we're wearing silk." I glanced down, but only to look at my own clothes.

A germ of an idea began to form. "Marta, can you take off your sash with one hand?"

"Are you mad? I can't let go of the spire! If you want to die, *you* let go of the spire!" She gasped for breath for a moment. "My hands are so sweaty right now, it's all I can do to hold on."

Which was another thing I'd been trying to ignore. My own hands were so wet that I was afraid to even think about them.

"If I start to slide," I asked, "will you at least use one hand to slow me down?"

"What?! Creel, what are you doing?"

Slowly, with my heart in my mouth, I loosened my right hand from the spire. My fingers were painfully cramped. As I opened them, I thought my left hand would let go as well, out of sympathy. I whimpered under my breath, both from pain and from the fear that what I was doing was very, very foolish.

"Creel, don't do it," Marta said.

"It'll work, I know it will," I said with feigned confidence.

My fingers all the way open, the entire weight of my body now hung from my left hand, which was shaking with the effort of hanging on. I tried not to hurry, but to move deliberately and smoothly as I untucked the end of my sash and loosened it.

When I at last pulled it off, the fine silk flapped in the wind and my numb fingers nearly lost their grip on it. Snatching it close to my breast, I stretched up with my right arm and tried to push one end around the spire.

"Creel, you're scaring me," Marta whimpered.

"Lift up one of your fingers, and hold this in place

for me," I told her. I didn't dare move a finger on my left hand, and I needed to reach around the other side of the spire with my right to pull the sash around it.

"No!"

"Marta, just do it!"

Still making little distressed noises, Marta shifted two of her fingers the barest fraction so that she could pinch the sash between them. This was enough for me to reach around the other side of the spire, catch the end of the sash, and pull it around.

When the ends hung even, level with my chest, I gripped them both firmly with my right hand. Then I took a deep breath and slowly let go with my left. As I started to slide down the roof, I grabbed the sash frantically with my left hand and held on for my life as I shot down the steep side of the turret roof. I screamed, and Marta joined in, until my weight nearly separated my arms from my shoulder sockets. I was clinging to the end of the sash with sweaty hands, my arms stretched high above my head, and still I couldn't feel the ledge beneath my feet. I tried to look, but without my sash my tunic had bunched up and all I could see was the white silk.

"Marta? Can you see how close I am to the ledge?"

"You're not dead?" was the muffled reply.

"Not yet. Can you look for me?"

"I'll try." Then, a moment later: "Oh! Stretch down your toes, you're only an inch away!" She sounded

surprised and also pleased. I doubted she could hold on
to the spire much longer herself.

I stretched down my toes and finally felt the ledge
beneath them, firm and wonderful. Letting go with one
hand and then the other, I rested my full weight on
the ledge of the roof. The relief as I lowered my tortured
arms brought tears to my eyes. Pressing my cheek to the
smooth copper roof, I leaned against it and savored the
feeling of having my arms at my sides and my feet on a
firm surface.

"I'm coming," Marta announced.

Looking up, I saw her take hold of the sash with her
right hand. She slid down a little, made a strangled noise,
then grabbed for the sash with her left and screamed as
she slithered down the roof, the silk sliding through her
grip with a speed that made me break out in a cold sweat
all over again.

With a thump she landed on the ledge beside me,
pulling the sash free of the spire with one hand. I took it
from her and shoved it into the waistband of my
trousers in case it came in handy again.

"Now what?" Marta's blue eyes were wide and she
was very pale.

"I don't know. I guess we wait for someone to see us
and help," I said. "We could try climbing down off the
ledge and into one of the windows." She paled even further and I added, "I'm not sure I have the nerve to try that
either."

The sun was now high in the sky and the heat that rose off the copper roof was unbearable. They must have servants mounted on dragons polishing the roofs every month, to prevent the copper from tarnishing, I thought.

We were stuck.

A gust of wind plucked at my clothing, and I pressed harder against the roof. Then it came again, this time carrying the scent of sulfur with it. I opened my eyes.

A bright red dragon hovered in the air to the side of our turret. Her golden eyes were wide with astonishment. I raised my head, noticing that her horns had been sawed off. It was the female Tobin had uncollared.

"It's you!" I said to her.

"Human maids, what are you doing here?" Her voice had a lilting accent. "This is not safe!"

"Krashath dropped us here," I said.

"Krashath!" Her eyes narrowed. "Where are the human males you were with, and the dragons who are your friends?"

"They don't know where we are, they're hiding in a cave to the north of the city. Can you tell them?"

"The wind is rising, you cannot stay on that little ledge much longer," she said. "Jump off and I will catch you."

"No!" Marta sounded near hysteria again. She had her eyes shut and wouldn't look at the dragon. "We don't know you! What if you're allied with Krashath?"

"Marta," I explained patiently. "This is the female

that Tobin freed. She's been fighting the collared dragons." I turned back to her, uncertain now that I had said
that. "Haven't you?"

"By the First Fires, of course I have! I've been ripping
the collars off any dragon I could reach!"

She flapped her wings to maintain her position, and I
squinted against the hot air that blasted into my face. She
was right: it was getting too hot and we were far too
tired. By the time she flew out and found our cave, spoke
to Niva and the others, and they came for us, we would
have fallen to our deaths.

I made a decision. "Will you fly below us, so that we
can jump onto your back, mistress?"

"Creel, are you sure?" Marta's voice was fainter now,
and I knew that she had to be as tired as I was.

"It's our only chance," I told her quietly.

"I'll have to fly out a ways and come back in fast so
that I can tuck my wings as I pass beneath you. It's the
only way I can get close enough. I'll call out when I'm in
position."

"All right."

"I'm not jumping backward," Marta said. "Let's turn
around."

Feeling the edge carefully with our feet, we managed
to turn ourselves so that our backs were against the roof.
Because of its steep angle and the jutting ledge, we
couldn't see anything below the ledge.

"If this doesn't work, at least we'll die quickly, of the

fall, rather than slowly from starvation," I said to Marta with a weak grin.

"You're horrible." She clasped my hand. "But I'm still your friend."

We heard the flap of dragon wings, and clutched each other's hand tighter.

"Now," came the female dragon's shout.

"Now!" Marta and I shouted together, and jumped off the roof.

Flamewing

The long ridge of plates that stood up along the dragon's spine got me right in the gut, knocking the wind out of me. I was just grateful that they weren't sharp enough to do any permanent damage, as Shardas's and Niva's were. Marta landed on her side, and then started to slither off over the dragon's scaly shoulder before she grabbed one of the spines and stopped herself.

"Are you all right?" The dragon called the question back over her shoulder as she soared away from the palace.

All I could do was groan, so Marta answered for us. When my breath came back, I scrambled around until I was sitting between two of the plates. Marta rode just in front of me, looking calm and natural as though she had ridden dragonback dozens of times. She sounded almost chipper as she directed our rescuer toward the hill that concealed our friends.

When we landed outside the grove of olive trees, I clambered off the red female's back with relief. I was tired of clinging to things and having my feet dangle terrifyingly far above the ground.

One of Luka's men came out of the grove, a cross-bow loaded and held at the ready. When he saw us standing beside the strange dragon, he lowered the crossbow and called over his shoulder that it was all clear.

Luka burst out of the trees and ran to us. He grabbed me by the shoulders and kissed me right on the lips. Then he wrapped both arms around me and squeezed until I felt like I'd had my wind knocked out again. Glancing over his shoulder, I saw Marta getting much the same treatment from Tobin.

For just a moment I let myself go boneless and lean against Luka's chest. Then I stepped back and straightened my braids with great decorum. My heart was beating almost as fast as it had when I slid down the roof.

"This was the stupidest, stupidest thing any of us has ever done," Luka was ranting. "We never should have let you go back into the palace. Junn and Fallon were in the Grand Market, and heard that the king's Feravelan tailors had been arrested. Amacarin and Niva are circling the palace right now with Fallon and Junn, looking for a way to rescue you. Tobin refused to let me go: I was beside myself, thinking you'd already been executed."

"You didn't see us hanging from the roof?" I was almost disappointed. Looking back, with my stomach churning, it had been quite a feat to first slide down the roof to the ledge, and then jump off onto the back of a strange dragon. Sadly, it rather made the sensation of being kissed by Luka pale in comparison.

"Hanging from the roof?!" Luka's face was gray.

"I found them clinging to the roof of a turret," the dragon put in.

"Thank you very much for saving them . . . mistress," Luka said, bowing to her.

"My name," she said with dignity, "is Anranria." She bowed her head, but at Tobin. "And I owe you my life, for taking that collar off my neck."

He nodded, and then signed that we should go inside the cave to avoid being seen. Anranria seemed hesitant at first, still wary of humans, but I assured her that we had other dragons to vouch for us.

"Well, just Feniul right now," Luka corrected me as we went inside. He was holding my hand uncomfortably tightly.

I stopped in my tracks, remembering what he'd said earlier. "Niva went to the palace? But won't they realize again that she's a female?"

"She said she would hold her tail and forelegs a certain way," Luka said vaguely. "Feniul and Amacarin seemed to agree that it would work."

"It will work. Niva is quite masculine, really," Feniul said as we entered the cool dimness of the cave. Then he saw who Luka was talking to. "Creel! Marta! Thank the First Fires!" He extended his forelegs to us, and Marta and I hastened to pat his nose and reassure him.

Then Feniul saw Anranria behind us, and straightened his entire spine, all the way to his tailtip. "How do you do, madam." This genteel greeting was somewhat ruined by Ruli, who was swinging from one of his horns and chattering at Marta in an accusatory way.

"Oh, a monkey! How precious," Anranria said. "I adore small mammals, don't you?" She extended a fore-claw to Ruli, who skittered onto her foreleg and then ran up to her shoulder.

"I am more partial to dogs," Feniul said. "Although I do find the monkey . . . amusing."

I snorted. Just yesterday morning Feniul had threatened to eat Ruli.

"Oh, dogs! I had a pair of sheepherding dogs before I was collared. They helped with my flock immensely."

"Ah, sheepherders! A fine breed," Feniul said with real enthusiasm. "And you kept your own flock of sheep? How industrious of you, madam."

"My name is Anranria Flamewing," she told him. "But you may call me Ria."

He puffed out his chest. "And I am Feniul the Green-Clawed."

"This is so darling," Marta whispered to me. "I think Feniul is smitten!"

"You know," Luka whispered on my other side. "I never noticed before, but he really is green all over. Down to the tips of his claws. All the other dragons I've seen have had different colored claws or horns or something."

"That's great," I said in a normal voice, startling

everyone. "But we have a little problem called Krashath and the Citatian army to worry about right now." Immediately, my harsh announcement raised a flood of guilt that reddened my cheeks. I was so relieved to be alive, to be back with Luka (and the rest of my friends) that I could barely stay on my feet. But at the same time, the feeling of Krashath's claws around my waist was haunting me. He had to be stopped.

Ria and Feniul shuffled their feet and looked as embarrassed as two large dragons can look. Tobin and Luka just looked grim.

"Well," Luka said. "We weren't sure what to do about the two of you, but we did decide what to do about the army."

"And that is?"

"Leave," Luka said. "I'm not happy about it, but there's nothing that so few of us can do against an entire army of dragons. Niva, Feniul, and Amacarin have agreed to help us fight, but we're going back to Roulain to make our stand."

"Roulain?" I raised my eyebrows. It had been only a year since they had tried to conquer us, so I wasn't all that concerned with their well-being. But Roulain, rife with busy ports, did lie between Citatie and land-locked Feravel. I supposed that the common folk didn't deserve to be trampled by an army of dragons simply because their previous king had wanted Feravel's rich wool and fur trade for himself.

"The shore will make an excellent fighting ground," Feniul said. "The Citatians won't have a place to land. We can flame at them as they try to pass overhead, and if they bring any ground troops in ships, the Roulaini army can help fight them."

"Do you think the Roulaini will?"

"Niva spoke to her mate in the pool this morning," Luka assured me. "Roulain doesn't want an army of dragons stampeding over them on their way to Feravel. Their army is mobilized, and I've given instructions for them to meet us at the beach in three days' time." He smiled thinly. "The new king is apparently a tad offended that his country is only an obstacle to conquering Feravel."

"I wish Krashath wanted Roulain instead," I said. "How will your father get word to them?"

"A dragon from Roulain named Teonnil has come forward," Luka said. "He has arranged for a speaking pool in the palace gardens, and transmits messages from Leontes and King Caxel to King Rolian."

"How amazing," I said, marveling that so many dragons had come forward to help. Not even two weeks ago I had been begging Niva and Feniul to accompany me to Citatie to help spy. Now they were planning a full-on attack, with the aid of dragons from Roulain and even Citatie, for Ria was offering her support and that of her uncollared friends.

"I've freed a few of my companions from the hatching

grounds," Ria told us. "They're in hiding right now, most of them. We don't dare travel too far until the army has left Pelletie, lest we be spotted by a patrol. I am sure that I can convince them to help fight Krashath, though."

"How did you know Krashath was behind this?" This had been bothering me since I heard her swearing at Krashath all the way from the palace to the cave. "The royal court doesn't even know that their king is under his control."

Her head drooped. "Some of us were born in captivity," she said. "But I and many others remember when Krashath came. I am from the country of Luriel, far to the east of here. Krashath came to our land some ten years ago. He tried to convince us to follow him: to overthrow our rightful king and any who supported him. He claimed to have been our late Queen Velika's true mate." She shook her head. "We refused and he fled. But months later, a few at a time, the dragons of Luriel began to disappear. Krashath ambushed us in our sleep, one at a time at first, and then more and more as he gathered slaves. How well I remember seeing torchlight gleaming on Krashath's scales as I was netted and collared like a wild animal, trapped by friends and neighbors I had known since I was a hatchling.

"We went to other countries, trapping other dragons and being forced to mate and bear eggs in horrible conditions so that his army might grow. When there were too many of us to hide, he came here to Citatie, and made his deal with the vizier. Then our control was transferred to the Citatian soldiers, under his orders. They hid us in the desert until a few weeks ago. It was a nightmare made real."

There was a long silence, and then Luka cleared his throat.

"How many of your uncollared companions do you think will join us?" His face was somber. "A dozen? More?"

"I have uncollared nine," Ria said. "Although two of them have hatchlings that they wish to protect, and one left a clutch of eggs behind. She is mostly concerned with getting her eggs to safety."

"Oh." Luka's disappointment was palpable.

"Still," I said brightly, "there're six more dragons, seven with Ria, who will help us. That's much better than the three that we had before."

"True," he agreed. "We'll need to leave tonight, as soon as the sun sets, so that we have enough time to cross the strait and make our stand on the Roulain coast."

"All right," I said. I sank back onto a cot, exhausted. "Can I sleep for a little while, then?"

"Me, too," Marta sighed. She was already sitting down, Tobin's arm around her waist, and her head resting on his broad shoulder. "I did spend the afternoon hanging from a roof." She patted Ria's foreleg. "Thank you for rescuing us."

"Yes," I said, also patting her leg. "Thank you."

A strange look came into Ria's eyes, and she sniffed at me, sucking my loose tunic away from my body. "You smell very strongly of a certain dragon. . . ." Her head drew back, and her eyes widened. "One I have not seen in many years." She sniffed me again before turning to Feniul. "She smells of the Gold," she said, her voice confused.

"Yes, she and my cousin are very close," Feniul said with pride. He made it sound as though he had introduced us.

"But we were told that the Gold had died, over a year past!" Ria's nostrils dilated. "So Krashath continues his plot against his brother. I did not believe him when he said Shardas lived. He said he felt it in his bones."

"Shardas *is* alive," Feniul assured her, "and on his way to fight Krashath." His dignified tone turned to worry. "Although he was badly hurt, and we are not sure that he is well enough yet to travel and to fight."

"The Golden King, alive!" Ria didn't seem to hear the part about his injuries. "And coming to defeat his brother at last! This is a great day! We must tell those I have hidden at once. Surely all nine of them will join us now. If only our queen were alive, to give us strength as well!"

"Oh, Velika's still alive, but she can't travel yet," Marta said. She was slumped across Tobin's lap and her eyes were shut. "Can I sleep now?"

She slept right through the torrent of questions that followed this pronouncement. And through our efforts to enlighten Ria about the situation with her queen and king. And through Luka sending one of his men with Ria and Feniul to gather up the other uncollared dragons and arrange a rendezvous point for that evening. She slept through Tobin kissing her cheek and arranging her more comfortably on her cot, and Luka trying to do the same for me, which made me blush and stammer and pull a blanket over my head to "shut out the light."

Then I slept as well, for the rest of the day, my mind and body far too tired to deal with any more excitement.

On the Shore

Nine dragons came from a cave to the south of the city. Nine dragons, gleaming in the moonlight, with bright eyes and silken wings. It was a wrench for three of them to leave their hatchlings and eggs, but they were excited at the idea of seeing their king, of fighting Krashath, and of being free once and for all.

Added to that nine were Ria, Feniul, Niva, and Amacarin, giving us a total of thirteen dragons with whom to fight. Once I would have cheered to have so many at my side. Once I would have laughed in awe and amazement. But that was before I had seen hundreds of dragons flying in formation above Nason's palace.

Across the Strait of Mellelie lay Roulain, and beyond that Feravel, but in the moonlight we could have been standing at the edge of the world. I leaned against Feniul's haunch to take off my slippers and empty some of the sand out of them. Hating the feeling of gritty feet crammed into shoes, I left them off, stuffing them into the top of one of the travel baskets that adorned Feniul.

"Niva and Amacarin are agreed: this wind is too

strong," Luka said, coming over to me. He leaned against Feniul, his arm just barely touching mine. "Dawn will be the best time to cross, the air will be clearer and they will be able to see a good place to land and make our stand."

He actually sounded eager, as though he thought we had a chance. On the flight from the cave to the shore, I had realized that all we were doing was looking for a good place to die. There was no way that we could defeat the army of Citatie with the meager forces at our command. Even if the Roulaini and Feravelan dragons joined us, how many could there be? During the Dragon War, I had seen perhaps twenty-five dragons all told, and several of them had not survived.

"You're awfully quiet," Luka said.

He couldn't see my face in the dark.

"This isn't going to work," I said. "They're going to slaughter us."

Putting an arm around my shoulders, Luka held me tightly. "It will be all right, Creel, you'll see. Shardas will meet us here, it will inspire the dragons. It might even force a few of the collared ones to resist the alchemy."

Wrinkling my forehead, I thought about this. Ria and Niva had told us that it was possible to resist, though it took all one's strength. But it would likely be little things, like refusing to flame someone, or changing direction just slightly to carry them away from the fight. Still, it might be enough.

But then I confided to Luka my deepest fear.

"What if Shardas doesn't come?" I clenched my fists just thinking of it. Because if he didn't, it meant that he was still too injured to fly. Or had done himself irreparable damage in the attempt. I said this to Luka as well.

Whipping his neck around so that his head loomed over us, Feniul breathed sulfur at us in shock. "How can you doubt Shardas?"

In the darkness I felt myself blushing. "Well, you've seen his wings. . . ."

"Shardas the Gold is our king because he is the strongest and wisest of us. He would not make a promise that he could not keep. He would not sit idly by while we suffered, fighting for our freedom."

"I understand that, Feniul. But he was angry and upset, and he may have misjudged how badly he was still hurt."

"Shardas wouldn't do that," Feniul said with simple conviction. "He'll be here in time, you'll see."

Wishing that I was as certain, I helped to unburden the dragons and we laid out bedrolls for the night. Lying in a hollow beside Marta, I slept like the dead until the first gold and pink light of dawn woke us.

As I stumbled about the beach, feeling muzzy and out of sorts, I squinted toward the far Roulaini shore. It was said that on a clear day you could see Roulain from Citatie, and vice versa. I supposed that the white line at the horizon was the Roulaini shore, with a fuzzy, dark smudge beyond it that was probably trees. And the glinting gold thing was probably . . .

"Shardas!"

The golden speck I had spied on the horizon was indeed a dragon, coming toward us in strange bursts of speed. We all gathered at the edge of the water to watch. I felt a range of emotions: joy, relief, anticipation. And then they were all pushed aside by a growing sense of concern. Something was wrong. He was listing from side to side with each flap of his wings and sinking toward the waves of the strait.

"Help him," I cried to the other dragons.

At once Amacarin and Feniul were in the air, speeding toward Shardas. On the beach, Niva began pushing at the sand with her tail, whipping it from side to side in great sweeps that nearly blinded me until I pulled the collar of my tunic up over my face.

"What are you doing?"

I heard the other humans around me crying out and rustling as they, too, covered their faces.

"Making a flat space for him to land," Niva said as though it should have been obvious. "Move aside, all of you."

I pulled my tunic down so I could see where I was moving to. I glanced out over the strait as I clambered up a small dune to get out of the way. They were much closer now, with Feniul on one side and Amacarin on the other. Shardas's wings were spread across their backs, and with their forelegs linked they were flying clumsily toward us. At first I thought it was the rosy light of dawn that changed the colors of their scales. Then I squinted, looking more carefully, and what I saw made my heart shudder in my chest.

Blood was dripping from Shardas's wings and running down the flanks of the two dragons that supported him.

"Marta, help me," I said, scrambling back down the dune to our baggage. "We'll need every cloak and tunic and scrap of cloth."

"He bleeds," Ria said in a wondering voice.

"Yes, he bleeds," I snapped, not in the mood for her awestruck expression. "Now help or get out of the way."

It seemed forever before the three male dragons skidded onto the beach. At once Feniul and Amacarin rolled out of the way so that Shardas could stretch his wings out and let them at last come to rest. I ran to his head, stroking the scaly muzzle I loved so well.

"You great fool," I said, my voice choked with tears.

"And a fine morning to you, too, Creel," Shardas said, his familiar rumble even rockier with pain.

"What have you done to your wings?"

"Nothing good, though I hardly dare to look," he said, heaving a huge sigh.

"Good morning, sir," Luka said respectfully, coming over. "Is there anything we can get for you?"

"A nice basket of peaches would not be amiss,"

Shardas said. "But I suppose there are none to be had in these parts and in this season." He chuckled, then coughed. "Some fresh water, perhaps."

One of the newly uncollared females grabbed up a barrel that we carried as a dragon drinking cup and went at once to the stream where we were getting our water. She filled the barrel and brought it to Shardas with humble apologies.

"What have you to apologize for?" He lowered his muzzle to drink.

"It should be finer," she mumbled.

"Nonsense," he replied after he had drained it. "What is your name, madam?"

"Gala, Your Majesty."

"Thank you, Gala. And you may call me Shardas."

"Shardas, this is all very nice," I hissed as Gala bobbed away. "But what are we to do with you? The Citatian army is going to be moving toward Feravel soon, and we were supposed to cross the strait today, to join with the dragons of Roulain on the shore you just came from!"

"And so you shall," he said, while around us the uncollared Citatian dragons murmured in shock at the way I was speaking to their king.

I saw Feniul dip his head to whisper something to Ria, who nodded thoughtfully. Probably telling her that I was quite mad, and so my foibles were tolerated.

"Prince Luka," Shardas said. "You will lead as many

dragons as you can assemble in a stand on the Roulaini shore. The area directly across from us would be an ideal place."

"Yes, sir," Luka said.

"Look to Niva as your second in command," Shardas added.

"I accept the duty, Shardas," Niva said. "But I must agree with Creel: you are in no state to fly, and lying here in the open you will be directly beneath the flight path of the Citatian army. Something must be done."

"As soon as I catch my breath, I shall continue on to Pelletie," Shardas said easily, as though Marta and Tobin weren't frantically piling our clothing and blankets over his wings in an effort to stop the bleeding.

"Why?" I was squeezing one of his talons as though I could heal his wounds through force of will.

"Because Krashath will remain behind," Shardas said complacently. "He will not dare come to Feravel to face me. That is why *I* came *here*. I will fight him, and kill him." He lifted his head to look at Luka again. "You need only hold your position until I have defeated Krashath," he instructed.

"Shardas, your wings are in tatters," I reminded him.

"Then I shall fight on the ground."

Letting go of his talon, I stepped away. Staring out at the water, I ran my thin braids through my fingers. He was worse than my brother, Hagen, at his most stubborn, worse than Luka. Shardas was determined to fight

Krashath, even if it killed him, even if his wings looked like shredded silk. . . .

I turned around and walked back to Shardas and Luka. I began to strip off the blankets that Marta had just put on his right wing. The damage was not bad: the bleeding had mostly stopped, and though the tears in the wing membrane looked raw and red, the wings were stronger than they had been when I had last seen them.

"Wing injuries bleed a great deal," Shardas said. "Even superficial ones."

"This is what we will do," I told them. "Luka, you will take the others to Roulain and make a stand as we planned. Amacarin and Marta will stay here with me and Shardas." Normally I would have wanted Feniul, ditherer that he was, but I hated to keep him from his new love, Ria. "We will get Shardas ready to fight Krashath."

"What are you hatching in that brain of yours?" Shardas tilted his head at me.

"Your wings are no good," I told him. "So I'm going to make you some."

All the Silk in the World

W ell, I can never go back to the Pelletie market,"
Marta announced as she slithered off Gala's back.

In the end, Gala had stayed with us instead of
Amacarin. She was anxious about her hatchlings and had
no experience fighting, whereas Amacarin enjoyed setting things alight. Marta began to untie the cords that
held bale after bale of silk on the dragon's back.

"Why?" I bit off a thread and held up the seam I had
just sewn to check for flaws. Satisfied, I laid it aside.

She blinked at me, as though looking for sarcasm in
the question. "Because only a crazy person buys ten full
bolts of gold silk on the same day," she said, after realizing that I was serious.

As I picked up another piece of silk and threaded my
needle, I had to admit she was right. When I had made my
trip to the market earlier in the day, I hadn't paid too much
attention to the stares I had gotten. But even I had seen the
wisdom of sending Marta for the second half of the silk.

"Well," I said, offering her some dim consolation.
"Do you really want to come back to Citatie after this?"

She shuddered and began sorting out the silk she had bought. While Marta sorted, I continued to sew together the carefully measured and cut pieces that I had been working on feverishly for most of the day.

We were encamped in a grove of the ubiquitous olive trees, just south of the beach where we had met Shardas. The trees were barely dense enough to cover the two dragons, who could not sit upright unless they first checked for any signs of dragon patrol. Luka and Tobin had been reluctant to leave us, but we had insisted: someone had to lead the Roulaini blockade, and the odds were that the average human soldier wouldn't take orders from a dragon. Besides, I had pointed out, neither Luka nor Tobin could sew, which meant they would only be getting in our way. I bit off another thread, and held my work up to Shardas.

"Stretch out your left wing," I ordered. "Gala, could you help me, please?"

She hurried to help as I spread the silk over the top of Shardas's left wing. My measurements had been correct, and the silk lay perfectly over the wing. It was not quite finished—there were still two sections of wing membrane to cover—but I had wanted to check the fit before I continued. I was trying to sew the silk so that the seams corresponded with the bones and joints of Shardas's wings; the smooth areas of silk would replace the missing membrane. As much as it pained me, I would be using the holes from the wounds in his wings to pass cord through and tie the silk down.

"Before you get much further, we'd better test this part," Shardas said. "Not just the fit, but how it feels when I fly."

"All right." I had sewn cords along the edges of the segments. Hands shaking for fear that I would cause more pain or do more damage, I slipped them carefully through the holes and tied them gently in place. The holes in his wings were healing, I assured myself. One day, his wings would be healed.

If Krashath didn't kill him tomorrow.

"Does that feel secure?"

He stretched the wing and then contracted it. "Yes."

"Does it hurt?"

He blew gently on my hair. "No, it doesn't hurt."

Then he moved a little away from me. Lifting his head cautiously above the tree line, he scanned the area for signs of a dragon patrol or wandering humans. When he saw that it was clear, he reared up onto his hind legs, stretching out both his wings and flapping them in the hot, still air.

The silk on the left wing cupped, dragging at him and making a flapping noise. My heart sank. This would not work.

Shardas folded his wings and crouched down beside me again. He didn't need to say anything, but gave me a sympathetic look as I began to untie the silk from his wing. To my embarrassment, I found myself near tears.

"That didn't look right," Marta said, coming over to us, bright red silk spangled with mirrors trailing from her hands. "It was catching the wind."

"Yes, thank you, Marta," I said, not caring how rude I sounded.

She opened and then shut her mouth, her cheeks coloring. "It was a good idea, Creel," she said meekly.

"It *was* a good idea, Creel," Shardas echoed. "But things will turn out all right, regardless. Krashath wants to fight me. If it means he has to stay on the ground, he will." He shifted position so that I could better untie the rest of my failed scheme.

"No he won't," I said, choking on tears. "He'll stay in the air and burn you to ash. He won't fight fair, Shardas, you know that."

"May I say something?"

We all looked at Gala, who hovered nearby. The light filtering through the olive leaves made her bronze scales glow. She really was a beautiful dragon. I rather thought that Amacarin had been giving her an admiring eye before he had left.

"Of course you may, Gala," Shardas said, ever polite.

"Perhaps if you put that cloth on the underside of his wings," she suggested. "Like a kite."

We all just looked at her for a moment.

"A *kite?*" Marta's fair brow wrinkled. "What's that?"

"Oh!" Gala shook herself. "I once lived in the Spice Isles," she explained. "Kites are common there. They are . . . constructions of cloth or paper on light frames that . . . glide on the air."

Still not really comprehending, I looked at the cloth that Marta and I held, and then at Shardas's wings. Gala seemed to know what she was talking about, but I couldn't picture it.

"I think I know what she means," Shardas said. "I recall seeing such things some years ago." He nodded his head slowly. "If the cloth were on the underside, it would catch the wind and be pressed against my wings properly." He paused. "Although if I were to backwing . . ."

But I had caught the idea now.

"We'll have to put silk on both sides," I said. "And fasten the front and back together tightly enough that there's no way for it to gape or catch."

"We can sew it all along the top edge," Marta said. Her eyes were bright, and I could see that she had caught the vision as well. "In fact, we should sew it while you're wearing it, Shardas, to make certain that it's as tight as possible."

"We'll be working all night," I said, shaking out my hand.

"If you will just show me where to cut," Gala said, losing some of her shyness, "I think I can slice the silks neatly enough." She extended one razor-sharp foreclaw.

"Beautiful," Marta said. "I've got it all marked out over here." She folded the mirrored silk she was holding with a snap, and laid it on a boulder.

"Oh, Marta," I said, in a much more cheerful mood. "Why did you buy mirrored silk? Won't it be too heavy?"

Marta put her hands on her hips. "I knew you'd say something about that, Creel, but the last merchant gave me such an odd look—he was Citatian—that I panicked and bought a bale of the red mirrored silk, too." She laid out a piece of silk for Gala, who had just made short work of cutting up the last bit Marta gave her. Marta snorted. "I feel like we've bought up all the silk in the world!"

"I know it's not your fault, but now Shardas is going to look all patchwork and—" I lowered my arms, looking down at the mirrored silk. "Marta!"

"What?" She laid out some silk cord for Gala to cut into lengths for the ties. "What's wrong now?"

"Can you imagine what it would look like if Shardas spread his wings in the Citatian sun, and *this* was sewn to the underside?"

I held up a bolt of scarlet silk spangled with tiny mirrors. Even with the trees blocking most of the sun, the cloth itself was bright enough to make my eyes smart, and the mirrors caught stray sunbeams and reflected them dazzlingly.

"If jealousy doesn't stop Krashath in his tracks," Shardas said, his voice rumbling with laughter, "he will go quite blind."

Dragons in the Moonlight

That night the Citatian army passed overhead. It took a very long time, during which we had to douse our lanterns and huddle beneath the olive trees. I draped Shardas in some dark blue silk I had bought, intending to make wings for Velika when this was all over. Even in the coldness of the desert moonlight, Shardas's golden scales emitted a warm glow. Most of the rough, burned scales had been shed, and other than the lacework of his wings he was looking in fine fettle.

"I hope Gala is all right," Marta whispered.

After the sun had gone down, and once she had done all she could to help us, Gala went to see her hatchlings. We warned her to be careful, not wanting her to be caught and re-collared. But it seemed that she knew how to get around the patrols to reach them. And with the army mobilizing, it was likely that there would be fewer patrols than ever.

"She's a lovely dragon," I whispered, as overhead the rushing of dragon wings filled the night.

"Do you think that she can abide dogs?" Shardas

stretched and then readjusted the silk over his neck. "I have been hoping to find a mate for Feniul for years."

"One of your kingly duties?" Marta's voice was sympathetic.

"A familial one." Shardas let out a little snort of laughter. "If I had to find a mate for every dragon in the world, I should have dived into the Boiling Sea centuries ago."

"Or asked me to harpoon you through the ear," I put in.

"Precisely."

"I think you can stop worrying about Feniul," I assured him. "Did you not see him making eyes at Ria?"

"Oh, really?" He was quite astonished. "She is a beautiful female."

"Yes, and she's quite stolen my monkey, Ruli," Marta said with a sniff. "He hangs from her horns constantly and won't give me the time of day anymore. In fact, he's gone with her now."

"Good riddance," I said. "Can you imagine if he got in a snit and shredded all this silk? Or decided to . . . relieve himself on it?"

Shardas shuddered. "By the First Fires, I cannot abide monkeys. If this Ria does like small, annoying animals, then she and Feniul will no doubt do very well together."

"She used to have sheepdogs," I told him. "Apparently, she also used to keep her own sheep."

"Really?" He sounded thoughtful. "Intriguing."

"Why? Eventually there had to be a dragon out there that likes the same things as Feniul. He isn't *that* odd."

Shardas laughed. "No, I meant intriguing that she kept her own sheep. She doesn't have to steal food from humans, then."

"Unless she wanted to eat something other than sheep," I said.

"Maybe she had an orchard, too, or a garden," Marta chimed in. "There's no reason why she couldn't have had one."

"Precisely," Shardas said. "There's no reason why any dragon can't be self-sufficient: grow his own fruit, keep his own animals."

"Except that humans would notice if the neighboring farm was run by a dragon," I said.

"Yes," Shardas said in a quiet tone. "If there were humans to notice."

I started to ask what he meant, but then we heard a dragon flying low overhead, and had to stop talking. We stayed huddled and silent for a long time, until we heard crashing and roars and saw bursts of flame light the sky.

Figuring that I would only be taken for some gaping local if anyone saw me, I ran out of the trees to see what was happening. Down near the beach, dragons were fighting in the air, flaming at one another and shrieking while their riders shouted insults and instructions.

Those that had riders.

In the light from the flames I could see white figures crouched on the backs of some of the dragons, but not others. Had Niva led our friends back across the strait? Why?

A dragon swooped down to land beside me and I lunged back to the cover of the trees. Then I heard Gala's voice calling my name and came back.

"Halloo? Creel?"

"Gala! What's happening?"

"I freed several of the other females," she said in a pleased voice. "They were all very angry, and we decided to nip at the heels of the army as it crossed the strait."

Shardas stuck his head out of the trees. "Is this wise?"

Gala's head drooped. "So many of them were angry," she murmured. "I could hardly stop them now. They ambushed the last regiment before it could cross the strait."

"I should help," Shardas said. He hulked closer to me, and I felt him crouch as though preparing to spring into the sky.

"No you don't!" I laid a hand on his foreleg. "Your wings are in bad enough shape as it is. You are certainly not going to fight. Remember: you're resting up so that you can defeat Krashath. Don't waste your energy on this."

Feeling him relax, I took my hand off his leg and stepped toward Gala. "Not that you shouldn't be proud of what you've done tonight, Gala. This is amazing! How many did you free?"

"There was only one guard on patrol and I freed at least seven of my fellow females before he came back. And one of the newly uncollared took care of the sentries, forcing the dragon to land and uncollaring him, while the others helped me free more. I lost count around thirty."

"Thirty! That's wonderful!"

"It doesn't compare to the hundreds collared in the army," she said modestly. "So I had better go and help." She got ready to take off but checked herself to lean down to me. "Creel . . . if anything bad happens to me . . . please take care of my hatchlings."

A lump in my throat, I readily agreed to raise them as though they were my own dragon-children, and she took off.

We sat in the darkness watching the dragons fight on and above the shore until nearly dawn. It was eerily beautiful: the flashes of fire, the roaring and crashing as the great scaled beasts came together and then parted. Like watching the gods dance.

And then, near dawn, Krashath came.

The pale gray light and waning moon were more than enough to see him by. White and menacing, appearing far larger than I remembered, he hung in the air between our grove and the shore where the fighting still went on. Filling his lungs with air, he roared so that the ground shook and leaves rattled down from the trees all around us.

The skirmishers froze. Dragons locked in fearsome struggle hung in the air, their wings flapping and their claws entwined, and stared at Krashath.

"What is this?" Krashath's voice hammered at my ears. "Why have you not crossed the strait with the rest of the army?"

"He's using alchemy," Shardas whispered. "To make himself look bigger and sound louder." His voice was ripe with disgust.

I put a restraining hand on his foreleg again. "Don't go out there," I begged him. "Wait until we are done with the silk wings."

"I will," he agreed reluctantly.

"Soldiers, land," Krashath shouted.

All the collared dragons dropped to the sands. For the first time I noticed other shapes there: in the darkness I had thought they were dunes, but the dawn was slowly revealing the slumped bodies of dragons. I could not say yet who was dead and who was merely injured, but my heart shuddered within me and I prayed to the Triunity to protect Gala and her newly freed companions.

The uncollared dragons hovered uncertainly in the air. I knew how they felt, exposed, perhaps even chastened. Blood dripped from wounds, and I strained my eyes to catch a glimpse of Gala's bronze scales. It was still too dim to tell, though.

Krashath was moving, his body writhing, and I heard

words in the dragon tongue spoken low. Shardas growled and pushed Marta and I to the ground, holding a claw over each of us protectively.

Peeking out between his golden talons, I saw one of the uncollared dragons level herself off. She opened her mouth wide, screaming and flaming at the same time, and charged Krashath. It was not, to my relief, Gala, but a beautiful maroon female with violet horns. Just before she reached Krashath, who appeared unaffected by her flames, the white dragon spread his talons, and a golden mist flew out and into the face of his red-scaled attacker.

She wailed and fell to the sands, and the mist spread out. As it reached each of the hovering dragons, they, too, screamed and fell to earth. I couldn't stand their cries, or the heartbroken sound of Marta sobbing nearby. I writhed out from under Shardas's claw and ran out of the grove.

"Go!" I shouted to those dragons that still had strength. They were ducking and weaving in the air to avoid the strange golden mist that sought their faces. The dragons that had fallen were still and silent, and it brought tears pouring down my cheeks. "Go!" I screamed. "Fly to Roulain, join Niva, go!"

A dozen or so wheeled and fled across the strait, the golden mist following them a little ways before the salt breeze dispersed it. I turned and ran east, away from Krashath but away from Shardas, too, lest the brothers meet before Shardas was ready. I heard the flap of

Krashath's wings and felt the wind of his flight on my back. Something soft and strange struck my side, and it felt as though a warm blanket were enveloping me. For a sickening moment I thought it was the golden mist, but there was no pain. Roaring, Krashath flew over and past, and then wheeled around and came back. His neck whipped from side to side, and though I was right below him, he seemed not to see me.

"Shardas!" he roared, and I covered my ears. "I know this is your doing! Come out and face me, you coward!" He flew over the trees of the little grove, raking their upper branches with his talons, but there was no movement from within.

Finally, a hesitant blue dragon rose up from the beach, his white-clad rider waving one hand. Krashath flew to meet them, anger apparent in the beat of his wings and the clenching and unclenching of his claws.

The soldier asked Krashath a question in Citatian, his imperious manner showing that he thought Krashath was being controlled by the king.

Krashath snarled something in reply; the only word I caught was "Feravel." With that, Krashath flew back toward Pelletie, searching the grove with hungry eyes as he passed.

The Citatian soldiers mustered the dragons that could fly and continued across the strait, abandoning wounded soldiers and dragons alike. Once the able-bodied had flown out of earshot the blanketlike fog that enfolded me dropped away, and Shardas came out of the trees with Marta at his side.

"Shardas—," I began.

"I do not wish to speak," he said curtly.

"Creel! Why didn't Krashath see you?" Marta rushed to give me a hug.

"I don't know," I said. Shardas ducked his head, looking beyond us, and I felt a niggling suspicion. "Perhaps alchemy is more common in their family than we were led to believe," I whispered to Marta. Her eyes wide, she just nodded.

"Let us help the wounded," Shardas said, and turned toward the beach.

Speaking Pool

We finished the silk wings just before noon.

The stitches were large and crude, but they would hold. As Shardas said, he wasn't going to be attending any balls, so he didn't need to look especially pretty. He did need to look impressive, though, at least to Krashath, who would hopefully not get close enough to see the stitches.

After our run-in with Krashath, I was more frightened than ever for Shardas, but Marta seemed strangely reassured. When Shardas was out of earshot, catching a wild pig for our breakfast, she confided her convictions.

"Shardas can use alchemy, too, Creel," she said. "You just disappeared, in plain sight. I could hear him saying something, but I didn't understand the words, and then you disappeared. You mark my words, he's going to use Krashath's own weapon against him."

"He did live with an alchemist for many years," I said as I sewed the last of the silk cords in place. "I suppose he might have learned a thing or two from Jerontin."

"Exactly."

Then Shardas came back, and we had to stop talking. He was particularly silent this morning. The scene on the beach had been grim: most of the dragons and all of the humans there were dead. Shardas had uncollared those dragons that were injured, and then he ordered them to care for one another. When they were well enough to fly they were to head back to the hatching grounds and uncollar the remaining females.

"We must look to the young," he told them, before going off to find food.

When he returned from the hunt he had two pigs, one for us and one for himself, since he would need a big meal to keep up his strength for the fight with Krashath. He roasted them with a slow gout of flame while I gave his scales a hasty going-over. I found only two damaged scales left, and pulled them off with ease. His spine ridges needed filing, but we had no file at hand to do the job.

"Leave them," Shardas said, his voice curt. "Eat your breakfast, Creel," he said in kinder tones. "Besides, they're sharper this way."

After our mostly silent meal, we fitted Shardas's new wings into place. On the upper sides they were mellow gold, because my original vision had been to match Shardas's natural coloring as closely as possible, in an attempt to conceal his injuries from Krashath. Red and gold cords tied the triangular panels to his wings, and the underside was the real glory: scarlet silk, brocaded with hundreds of tiny mirrors.

"I feel like one of the temple fan-dancers of fabulous Dhair," Shardas said, amusement coloring his voice for the first time since last night.

"One of the what?" I looked up from the cord I was tying.

"Dhair and its fan-dancers were destroyed well before your birth, I'm afraid," he said.

Marta and I stepped back, and Shardas stretched and flapped to check the fit. The silk stayed in place, even as he twisted and rose off the ground a few inches.

"I'll try a flight," Shardas said, and launched himself into the air almost before we could step back.

Running out of the grove of olives, we watched as he circled high above us. From beneath, his wings looked . . . different, patterned scarlet, but the mirrors were not as impressive as I had hoped. Then Shardas hovered, back-winging, and tilted himself until the undersides of his wings were fully exposed to the sun.

It was blinding.

The intense sunlight of Citatie struck the mirrors and light flared out from Shardas's wings until we could not bear to look. Shielding our eyes, we watched in wonder as he spun and dove, playing with the light and the mirrors on his wings. At last he came back toward us, but did not land.

"Thank you, Creel. Thank you, Marta," he said, floating above us.

"You're not going, are you?" My voice sounded high and childish.

"I must. I must make use of the sun, and these wonderful silk wings you have made me." His blue eyes looked down kindly at us. "Go to the shore and see to the wounded dragons. One of them will surely be able to fly you home to Feravel in a day or two."

"But we want to go with you," Marta said, before I could. I nodded my agreement.

"No. Go home. And if you should see Velika again . . . watch over her for me." Then he wheeled and left us.

We stared after him in disbelief.

"He's going to fight Krashath alone," Marta said dully. Then she shook herself. "There's nothing we can do to help now, but still. I just thought we would be there . . . to at least see . . ." Her voice trailed away.

"I'm not going to sit here and wait for some strange dragon to take me home," I said. I took her arm and began to lead her to the beach. "Come along."

Picking our way around the bodies of fallen dragons was not pleasant, but neither was not knowing how Shardas was faring. Or Luka and the others. Never far from my mind was the fact that, across the strait somewhere, Luka was fighting an army of dragons at least four times the size of what we had been able to muster.

The injured dragons were huddled near the stream of fresh water. I strode purposefully over to the largest of them, who was also the least injured. I suspected that he had chosen to land on the beach and feign more mortal wounds as the only form of protest a collared dragon could make. He had a broken foreleg, and a long gash on his chest, but he was sitting up and giving instructions to the others when we approached.

"Good morning," I said in Feravelan. He had been speaking Citatian, but I counted on him speaking most human tongues, as the other dragons of my acquaintance did.

"Good morning, humans," he said. He was a trifle wary, and looked us over as if to see if we were concealing any collars about our persons.

"I'm Creel, this is Marta," I said, trying to look reassuringly un-Citatian. "What's your name?"

"Darrym." Still the wary look.

A dragon with a ruined wing beside us began edging away.

"Shardas the Gold has gone to fight Krashath, the white dragon who is controlling the human king of Citatie," I announced. "We came here to help him, but now we need your help. Can you make a speaking pool for me?"

"I can." He tilted his head and looked at me out of one green eye. He was mostly brown, with a greenish pattern of streaks along his sides and the membranes of his wings. "Who are you going to bespeak?"

"Queen Velika."

The dragons gasped and muttered at this, but I ignored them, raising my voice to be heard. "We must tell her what Shardas is doing and ask her advice." She knew Krashath as well as Shardas did, I was guessing, and might know a trick we could use to help defeat him. "We must also look in on Niva and the others fighting the collared army on the Roulaini shore."

"The queen lives?" The dragon with the ruined wing stared.

"She lives," I confirmed. "We must tell her where the king has gone."

"Well." With his good foreleg Darrym picked at the moss packing the wound on his chest. "Well. I see. Er." He lashed his tail and stretched his wings. "And, er, after that, do you need anything?"

"Yes." Marta was poking me and pointing to the perfectly healthy wings he had just displayed. "If you would be so good as to fly us to Pelletie as soon as Creel bespeaks the others?"

"Well, all right," Darrym said, looking taken aback. "I suppose I could."

"Don't listen to them, they just want to collar us," said a lithe lavender dragon. Lying on her side, she held one wing awkwardly away from a gaping wound that ran down her side from foreleg to hind. Another dragon was packing it with moss, and the lavender winced at every touch of her nurse's claws.

"They don't look like Citatians," Darrym said. "And they were with Shardas the Gold earlier, while you were still unconscious."

The lavender continued to mutter, and I gave her a hard look. The muttering stopped and I turned back to Darrym. "The speaking pool, if you please."

Darrym got to work. He dug a small inlet on one side of the stream and dammed it off when it had filled. He leaned over, intent, for no more than a moment before turning to me.

"Shall I invoke her majesty?" His voice was awed.

"Let me," I said. My voice was less crisp and more kindly now. "She is not accustomed to strangers."

Leaning over the pool, I called to Velika. With Marta hovering at one side and Darrym at the other, it was hard not to be self-conscious. The pool clouded, then cleared to show the interior of Velika and Shardas's cave, but it was empty. It clouded again, and remained that way.

"What does that mean?" I looked up at Darrym.

"She is not in her cave," he said. "She is not within the sound of your voice."

This caused me some confusion. I had called quite loudly, and the cave was not large. Surely even if she were sunning herself outside, she would have heard me? I felt panicky at the thought that Velika might be injured. Where were Niva's hatchlings? They were supposed to be helping her!

"Creel." Marta jogged my elbow. "We'd better just check on Tobin and the others and then get to Shardas. There's no time."

Knowing she was right, yet disturbed all the same, I

called for Niva, then Feniul and Amacarin. It was Ria who at last appeared in the pool, though.

"Hello, young Creel," she said in her sensible voice. "How fares our king?"

"He is as well as can be expected, Ria. But he has gone to fight Krashath, and we are worried."

"By the First Fires, I hope he succeeds," she said. "A terrible thing, if Krashath were to defeat him. But if Shardas the Gold wins, we shall win as well." Her voice turned grim: "Otherwise, I doubt we have much hope."

"Is it bad?"

"It is very bad," she said. "We are holding steady, but they outnumber us and even those who came at dawn are not enough to turn the tables completely."

"Is Tobin all right?" Marta leaned over the pool.

"The hairless man with the markings on his head?"

"Yes, he is my betrothed."

"He is a mighty fighter," Ria said with admiration. "He can throw a javelin with such skill that he strikes the dragonriders straight through the heart. But the riderless dragons mill about, getting in the way, and it is difficult to get close enough to uncollar them."

"Is Gala there?" I had not seen her bronze form among the fallen dragons.

"Yes. She is injured, but she chased one of the col-lared dragons all the way across the strait." Ria looked over her shoulder and then back. "I must go. I am needed." She started to withdraw, then came back. "Oh, dear Ruli is quite safe," she assured Marta, then the image rippled and she was gone.

"I hadn't even thought about that little monkey running around in the battle," Marta admitted. "I hope he isn't too frightened."

"I'm sure he's happily flinging . . . um, waste at the enemy," I told her. Then I went to Darrym, who was waiting nearby. "Please take us to Pelletie now," I said.

"At once." And he bent his good foreleg for us to mount.

"How are we going to help Shardas?" Marta asked when we were in the air.

"I don't know," I said. "But I can't just sit here."

"I agree," she said, and Darrym arrowed toward the city, the afternoon sun beating down on us.

Wings of Scarlet, Wings of Gold

M y hopes soared as Darrym flew over the palace.

We had circled the city, approaching the palace in ever-smaller loops so that we wouldn't be in Shardas's way. We could see him, gleaming in the sun with his brilliant silk-covered wings, from a great distance. But we did not see Krashath until we were almost directly above him.

White like the underbelly of a cave fish, he huddled on the roof of the Citatian royal palace, twined around the spires at one end of the main building. Not wanting to disturb the fine balance between the two fighting brothers, I ordered Darrym to land on the roof of the palace a ways away. Darrym crouched behind a squat tower, and we all leaned around to watch the fight.

From our position we could see why Krashath huddled on the roof, his dead black eyes half-closed. Shardas was carefully hovering in the air just so, and whenever Krashath raised his head, Shardas would tilt his wings so that the sun struck his brother full in the face. Most dragons are not bothered by the sun in their eyes, at least, not the way humans are. But Krashath had spent many long hours in the throne room, crouched in darkness, and now he ducked his head and blinked whenever Shardas moved.

"The sun will set, Shardas," Krashath hissed. "If you have not the courage to kill me by then, I will have no qualms about ripping out your throat."

"Recall your army, Krashath," Shardas countered. "What you are doing is wrong, and you know it. Recall them."

"I will destroy you, and everything that reminds me of you, Shardas," Krashath said. "I will not rest until Feravel is a wasteland. It's taken me centuries to recover my strength, but I am more than ready to crush you now."

"I wonder if he would say that if he knew Velika was there," Marta whispered. "If he knew it would destroy her, too."

I sat up straighter on Darrym's back, ready to give the order for him to fly in closer.

"Absolutely not," Darrym whispered, twisting his neck to look over his shoulder at us. "I know what you are about to ask, but this is as close as we get. Call me a coward if you want, but I've spent fifteen years with a collar around my neck because of Krashath, and I'm not going any closer."

"This is why you are not king, Krashath!" Shardas bellowed.

"I am the king of Citatie," Krashath said, laughing evilly. "That fool in the room below us cannot even dress himself without me. And when I have conquered Roulain and Feravel, I shall be ruler of all the dragons of the north! Then nothing will stop me from ruling over all our kind!"

"That is why she did not choose you, Krashath," Shardas said. "She never would have chosen you! You have no soul."

"*Do not speak of her!*" Krashath screamed. He half-rose, snarling at Shardas with his eyes squeezed shut against the light.

"He's mad," Marta and I said at the same time.

"Oh, quite," Darrym agreed.

"Do not dare to speak of her to me!" Acid spittle flew from Krashath's muzzle and sizzled on the roof tiles. "You stole her from me! You poisoned her against me! I hate you!"

He launched himself at Shardas, who dodged him easily. Krashath had lunged with his eyes still closed, but he opened them now, for Shardas had been forced out of the line of the sun, and he had to beat his wings rapidly to avoid Krashath. Now they fought as dragons normally did: with fire and claw and fang.

Clinging to each other, Marta and I huddled on Darrym's back. I could feel him shuddering beneath us. We had seen dragons fight before, just last night even, but this was something else.

Krashath and Shardas were the largest dragons I had ever seen, and they fought with a passion and viciousness that was unrivaled. Perhaps, I thought, it was because they were brothers, and had once loved each other, that they hated so deeply now. Their roars shook tiles down off the roofs and their tails knocked holes in stone walls. A stray burst of fire from Shardas melted the copper roof on a tower not far from us, and Darrym slithered along the ridgepole to the next turret, and then the next, to stay out of their path.

Shardas flew into position once more, flashing his silken wings into Krashath's eyes. As his brother screamed and flailed, trying to avoid the brilliance of the mirrors, Shardas whipped around and raked Krashath's belly with the long ragged spines of his tail. Krashath blew out a great gust of fire, mostly from the shock of the pain, and one of Shardas's silk-covered wings caught fire. Shardas ducked down and raced in a circle below Krashath, putting out the fire with the wind of his passage, and Krashath chased after him, roaring.

Raking at Shardas's wings with his black claws, Krashath caught the charred silk and ripped some of it away. Shardas twisted his head and bit through the cords that held the cloth in place and then snapped it over Krashath's head.

Blinded, his head and one foreleg wrapped in silk, Krashath flew into one of the towers. With a scream he fell from the sky, landing atop a thick wall of stone that his weight instantly reduced to rubble. He burned the silk to ash and scrambled to his feet just as Shardas bore down on him again.

I thought at first that Shardas was badly injured because of the way he held his still-covered wing, but then I saw what he was doing. As he glided down to his brother, he held the wing twisted upward to catch the sun, beaming light directly into Krashath's eyes so that he could not see as Shardas landed almost on top of him and ripped at his throat with long golden claws.

Krashath's screaming was terrible. Even with my ears covered, I feared I would go deaf. He thrashed and writhed, destroying a whole wing of the palace in his death throes.

A patrol of Citatian dragons and soldiers arrived, probably the lone formation left behind to guard the hatching grounds, but they didn't know what to do and merely circled above us, roaring and shouting in frantic futility.

From our vantage point on a narrow peak of roof, I could look back over my shoulder and see the main doors of the palace. People were fleeing in droves, their arms burdened with children or bundles of clothes or, in one strange case, a large ham. I sent up a prayer to the Triunity that everyone had gotten out of the eastern wing of the palace before Krashath's thrashing had brought it tumbling down.

Shardas leaped away from his brother, coming to

land on a tower not far from us. He saw us for the first time, and called something to me, but my hands were still too tight over my ears for me to hear.

Krashath's screams were making me physically ill. I glared at Shardas, willing him to go to his brother and end his pain, but he was gazing beyond us, beyond the palace. Marta turned to look where he was looking. Her arms, squeezing my ribs, tightened further, and I turned to see what had captured their attention. Seeing nothing, I looked back at Krashath, praying silently for him to die.

And then Velika was there, and everything seemed to stop.

Seeing her float above the ruin of the palace, I understood why Krashath hated his brother so. She was magnificent: azure blue, with horns of silver like a crown and an elegance of form and movement that I had never before had a chance to appreciate. The last of her burned scales had been removed, and her new scales gleamed.

To my surprise I saw that her wings were almost healed. Where Shardas's still had holes throughout, she had only patches of rose-pink membrane that looked to be tender but still serviceable.

She hovered above the wreckage for a heartbeat before circling down to land beside Krashath. His cries had been growing fainter, and his writhing less frantic, and when she lighted beside him, he ceased altogether. He was still alive—the sudden silence was filled with his ragged breaths—but he lay in a relatively calm state and looked at her with his flat black eyes.

"Krashath," she said in her rough-soft voice. "Krashath, it should not have come to this."

"Velika," he gasped. "Velika, I . . . wanted . . ."

"You wanted power, more power than any dragon should have," she chided gently. "And you have paid the price for it."

"No!" The word was wrenched from his soul.

"Yes." She laid her foreclaws gently on his. "Rest now, Krashath. Go into the Eternal Sun."

His eyes closed, and I thought he had passed into death at last. There were tears coursing down my cheeks, and Marta's, too, I saw. He seemed a pitiful thing now, desperate and broken. His eyes opened again, and I gave a little gasp.

"Velika? Did you ever . . . love . . . me?"

She leaned in close and whispered to him so that none of us could hear. Then his eyes closed a final time, and his body sagged as the powerful spirit within it at last fled.

Getting Proof

Somehow I expected that it would all be over once Krashath was dead. The Citatian army would return, the dragons would rip off their collars, and we would all dance in the moonlit streets of Pelletie.

But nothing happened after Krashath died, save that Shardas went to Velika. She raised her head to keen the dragon mourning song, and Shardas looked at her for a moment or so.

"I am not sure that he deserves this," Shardas said. But a moment later he joined her.

The dragon patrol flew down to land in the rubble-strewn courtyard, and the soldiers dismounted and began shouting at Shardas and Velika. The human voices were too thin to carry up to our turret, and at last I convinced Darrym to fly down.

He bowed in the dragon fashion to Shardas and Velika—head down, forelegs primly together—then looked away as though Krashath's body was not there. He did not join the mourning rites, and I could hardly blame him.

Marta and I slipped off his back and went over to the commander of the dragon patrol, who was shouting at all of us in Citatian. I waved my arms until I got his attention and he realized that I couldn't understand him.

"What . . . happening?" His Feravelan was labored. "Why . . . no collar?" He pointed at Shardas and Velika.

"That," I said majestically, pointing to Shardas, "is the *king* of the *dragons*." I waited until I saw confusion give way to shock. "Yes, the *king*. Very angry king. No more collars!"

The patrol commander was aghast. He looked from me to his dragon to Shardas and Velika. They were both very large, and gleamed beautifully in the afternoon sun. Additionally, Shardas's unfiled spine ridges gave him a warlike appearance, and though he sang the mourning song with fervor, he was watching the commander out of the corner of his eye.

"No collar?" The man swallowed hard.

"No. No collar."

Marta shook her head adamantly and then drew a finger across her throat for emphasis. "No collars ever!"

The commander shifted from foot to foot for a moment, but then he gathered his resolve. "No! King Nason say collars." He pointed up at the throne room, some three stories above us. The wall overlooking the courtyard was missing, courtesy of Krashath's hasty exit with me and Marta in tow just three days prior. A board had been nailed across the hole.

"We'll see about that." I went to Darrym. "Lift me up into the throne room," I ordered.

"Me, too," Marta insisted.

Just then the mourning song for Krashath faded away into silence. Velika and Shardas rounded on us immediately.

"What are you doing?" Shardas's eyes flashed: Darrym had a foreclaw around my waist and was reaching for Marta.

"They said to lift them. . . ." Darrym trailed off.

"Creel," Shardas said. "This is too dangerous."

"We need Nason and Arjas to help us stop this war," I said reasonably.

"I'll get them."

"How? You're too big."

"There must be a way to—"

Tense with anxiety, I said, "Shardas, we have to get Arjas and Nason to Roulain to call a stop to this war. The Citatian army doesn't know that Krashath is dead, and they didn't know that he was controlling the king. We're going to need solid proof to convince them to stop their advance on Feravel."

"We spoke to Ria before we came here," Marta chimed in. "They cannot win without our help."

"Then we must go at once," Velika said. She extended her wings, one at a time, to look at the healed patches. Up close the pink patches did look somewhat raw, but far better than Shardas's wings. She clucked over them, concerned.

"We don't have time to fit you with silk wings like Shardas's, I'm afraid," I told her. Gala had cut out the pieces of silk, but that was as far as we'd gotten with the blue wings. There had not been enough time to sew them, and I saw now that there were no holes in her wings to pass the ties through anyway.

"There is some discomfort, but the flight will not be unbearable," she decided.

At last Shardas nodded to Darrym, who lifted us up and over the rail and onto the marble floor of the throne room. Then he gripped the edge of the floor with his forelegs so that he could see us clearly, and I saw Shardas and Velika stretch up to watch on either side. Drawing my belt knife, I looked around the room.

It was empty, as I had expected. I started toward the large double doors that led into the rest of the palace, but Marta stopped me with a hand on my arm.

"Listen," she whispered.

Freezing, we listened until I felt my ears straining away from my head. Then we heard it: a low sobbing sound that was quickly muffled. It was coming from a small door, half-hidden by a silk hanging behind the throne, where Krashath used to lay.

We crept toward the door, followed by a barely audible rumble from Shardas, warning us to be careful. I went first, opening the door a crack and peeping into the room beyond, Marta breathing down my neck, and my knuckles white on the handle of my knife.

The room was a retiring chamber with a couple of low couches and a round table. On one of the couches lay a figure I thought was the king. It was hard to tell because his head was covered with a pillow that was being firmly held in place by Lord Arjas. The king's legs kicked feebly, and I threw the door open and leaped into the room.

"Stop that!"

Arjas looked up in surprise, but didn't remove the pillow.

"I said stop!" I shouted, and lunged at him.

Marta and I both attacked him, stabbing him with our little belt knives and screaming like vengeful ghosts. I could hear Shardas bellowing, demanding to know what was happening, but there was no time to respond. While Marta, who I had to admit was a better fighter than I, gave the vizier a long gash down one arm, I wrestled the pillow from his hands and freed the king. Nason slid onto the floor and lay there gasping like a landed fish.

Furious at not being able to see, Shardas finally tore the entire inner wall of the throne room down, exposing us like actors on a stage to the gazes of the three dragons. The king screamed as the light streamed in, and crawled under a couch. Shardas reached in and grabbed Arjas, who was struggling to draw his own knife, and pulled him out of the room to dangle above the courtyard.

"Who are you?"

Arjas could only gabble and kick, robbed of speech by this cavalier treatment by an angry dragon.

"That's the vizier, Lord Arjas," I told Shardas. "This one is the king." I grabbed his ankles and dragged him out from under the couch.

"I'll get him," Darrym said cheerfully. He plucked King Nason from the room and held him up to his face. "Good afternoon, Your Majesty," he sneered.

"Don't taunt him," Velika ordered. "He's clearly near breaking down."

"Also, he was already a bit simple," I said. Marta and I went to the edge of the room and Shardas moved around so that we could climb onto his shoulders.

"This explains how Krashath got a hold on him," Shardas said.

There was anger and pain in his voice, and I realized that, as much as we had all wanted—needed—Krashath to be eliminated, it had caused great turmoil for Shardas. I thought about how I would feel if I had to kill my own brother—Hagen would never hurt a soul, of course— but if I *had* to or thousands of people would die. It wasn't something I wanted to contemplate for long.

"We must go quickly," Velika said. "I flew wide around the battle, but even from a distance it was a terrible sight."

Marta and I settled ourselves on Shardas's back, and he launched himself into the air. Velika, with Arjas in her claws, and Darrym with Nason, followed soon after.

"How is it that your wings are not as badly damaged from the flight as Shardas's?" Marta called the question to the queen dragon before I could.

"I left not long after he did, but flew slower and with more rest," she explained. "Also, I am not averse to the use of alchemy."

Giving her a sharp look, Shardas said, "Leontes?"

"Indeed."

"Niva's mate?" I asked. "He's an alchemist?" I was longing to meet the dragon who could stand to be mated—for life!—to stern Niva.

"He dabbles," Velika said. "He offered to try a healing potion on both of us when he first arrived with the hatchlings, but Shardas refused on behalf of both of us." She gave him a sidelong look. "As soon as your tailtip disappeared over the horizon, I drank the potion, then escorted the hatchlings and their father to the King's Seat."

"That was your choice," Shardas said with equanimity.

"And I do not regret it."

Twisting around, I exchanged amused looks with Marta. She had not spent as much time as I had around Shardas, and I would hardly dare to say that I knew Velika at all well, but I could see by her expression that this was refreshing to both of us. Shardas and Velika were bantering, in the wry, humorous way of the dragons, precisely like an old married couple. It cheered my soul to hear them like this, after their many years of separation and pain.

"Shardas can use alchemy," I called to Velika. "He made me invisible yesterday."

"Did he?" She gave her mate an arch look. "A nice trick."

Shardas simply hummed to himself in a vibrating rumble that tickled my legs and made Marta giggle.

"But you wouldn't accept a healing potion from Leontes?" I would have taken the potion in a heartbeat, especially if I were facing a long flight followed by a long fight.

"I do not trust the alchemy of others," Shardas said reluctantly, after a long silence. We all nodded, understanding perfectly.

Despite the panel of silk that had been ripped off his wings by Krashath, and many small injuries, Shardas flew like an arrow toward the strait. Velika and Darrym flanked him, and I was pleased to see that Darrym, though in better health, had trouble keeping up. Of course, he was carrying the Citatian king in his foreclaws, but Nason hardly moved during the entire flight.

Arjas, on the other hand, screamed and thrashed for all he was worth. Velika soared on, ignoring the screeching human in her claws. In this fashion we proceeded to the Strait of Mellelie.

Citatie's Mighty Army

The Battle of the Mellelie, as it came to be known, was a grievous thing. It extended into the air above the strait, and the hot dragon blood dripping down into the water sizzled and steamed. It reminded me uncomfortably of the last great battle I had seen, above the Boiling Sea, which had ended with the supposed deaths of Shardas and Velika. Nothing in the Dragon War or in last night's skirmish on the beach had prepared me for this, though. A multitude of dragons were locked in combat, so many that I could not begin to count them. The roaring and screams were deafening, and too often there was a great splash as a dragon fell into the water and did not resurface.

Those dragons who fought over the shore risked taking an arrow or lance from the humans on the ground. The Roulaini forces were massed behind hastily piled sandbags, firing volleys of arrows in an attempt to hit either a soft place between dragon scales, or a Citatian soldier. This made me wince, however: the fighting dragons moved with such speed and violence that there was no way to determine if an arrow, once shot, would hit a collared dragon or a free one.

There was a group of dragons clustered together on the ground behind the ranks of human soldiers that confused me. They did not appear injured, they were not collared, and yet they did not fight. They just huddled there, looking forlorn and rather useless.

"Who are they?" I pointed them out with an imperious finger. We needed every able-bodied dragon we could find.

"See the collars? They must have been uncollared, and now refuse to fight," Darrym said, gesturing at a stack of the collars beside those dragons.

"Why wouldn't they want to fight back against the people who collared them?"

"Those aren't the people who collared them," Velika said. "Those are other dragons, their friends and family. I cannot blame them for not turning around and clawing out the eyes of their fathers and brothers."

"Some of them seem very young," Darrym added. "It's likely that they were born into the collar." He pointed to one small green dragon. "He's maybe two years old, probably just reached his full growth."

"Hold tight, ladies," Shardas said.

We were now close enough to the battle to have been noticed by the fighters. An uncollared dragon headed our way, claws extended in a threatening posture, and I realized that since we had come from the Citatian side, and were humans aboard Shardas, he assumed us to be the enemy.

"Stop," I shouted, just as Shardas did the same.

Shardas's voice drowned mine out, though. He drowned out the sound of the battle, the screams of combatants, and the crash of scale meeting scale. His voice was so loud that I clapped my hands to my ears and worried that the vibration would cause me and Marta to fall right off his back.

"More of his own alchemy?" Marta whispered into the silence that followed.

I nodded.

Many of the embattled dragons did freeze, and in the quietness I heard a human give the order for the archers to make a halt. Shardas's lungs filled for another alchemy-boosted bellow, and I squeezed with my legs and put both hands over my ears in readiness. Behind me, I could feel Marta hunkering down as well.

"Krashath is dead," Shardas shouted.

Despite my preparations I nearly slid sideways off his back. I had to take my hands off my ears and grip the spine ridge in front of me, so I shook my dozens of thin braids down over each ear, in vain hope that they would provide some buffer against that voice.

"The king of Citatie is here," Shardas went on. "Driven mad now that the dragon who controlled him is gone. Army of Citatie, surrender."

Darrym obligingly held up the gibbering King Nason.

We had the attention of the entire army now. Those who couldn't see us were being nudged and shouted to by their neighbors, and we looked out on a sky awash with bloodied dragons and frantic Citatian soldiers.

Then they attacked us.

The first rank of collared dragons, under orders from their riders, disengaged from their Feravelan and Roulaini opponents and came toward us with claws out-stretched. Bellowing for Velika and Darrym to get their prisoners to safety, and for Marta and me to hold tight, Shardas flew forward to meet them. On his back, my friend and I clung like burrs, and I'm ashamed to admit it, but I had my eyes shut.

I heard the *whoosh* of flames, but felt no heat, and dared to open my eyes a crack. Shardas had incinerated the first of our attackers, and was drawing breath for another burst of fire. I saw Darrym streak by, above and to one side, as he flew over the Citatians to make for the safety of the ground defenses with King Nason. Velika flew below us at the same time. Shardas whipped his tail around to strike an opponent with the barbed tip before that dragon could pursue Velika.

Another dragon charged us from above, and Shardas swerved and came around, fire blazing. His attacker screamed, and raked at Shardas's wings with his claws before falling, aflame, into the sea below. Another dragon came at us then, and another, and another. Shardas fought them all as he had fought his brother: with fang and claw, and with fire, while Marta and I clung to his back and tried to make ourselves the smallest targets possible.

But there were simply too many of them.

I saw Velika and Darrym fight their way to the sand-bag fortress, surrounded by a guard of free dragons, to deposit their prisoners. Then my view of the shore was obscured by a wall of dragons, all intent on destroying Shardas, who dove and twisted to avoid their fire, shouting for them to surrender.

And then.

Marta put her hands on my shoulders and gave them a little squeeze.

And then.

Marta used me for support as she stood up.

And then.

Marta leaped from Shardas's back.

She landed spread-eagle atop the Citatian soldier on our nearest attacking dragon. Marta stabbed the man with her belt knife, scrambled over his body before he stopped moving, and grabbed the leather collar around the dragon's neck. With a vicious slice, she severed the collar and let it fall free.

The dragon dropped out of the sky like a stone, silent and heavy as if it had been struck dead. Its rider, dead in actual fact, was still attached to the riding harness and hung limp on its back just behind Marta.

Who was getting ready to jump off again.

Seconds before the uncollared dragon hit the water, Marta leaped from its back to another dragon that soared underneath just in time.

It was Feniul.

Feniul, his claws and tail actually dragging in the water of the strait, arrowed below the falling Citatian dragon and caught Marta on his back as smoothly as though they had rehearsed the move. She shouted an order to him, and he took her up, up, up, before tilting so that she could jump onto yet another Citatian soldier. She pulled yet another knife from some concealed place—a trick I had no doubt Tobin had taught her—but this soldier surrendered, and sat with his hands in the air while she removed his dragon's collar.

"Well!" I refused to be shown up by Marta.

Clambering to my feet, I crept over Shardas's shoulder, and he, anticipating my need, gave a little dip and roll that bounced me into the air. I landed right on the neck of another dragon, and got the collar off before his rider could react.

Looking down, I saw a familiar bronze-scaled back, and leaped backward onto Gala, who took me up and under a Citatian dragon. I uncollared that one from Gala's back, and he pitched his rider into the sea with a bellow of pure joy.

Looking around for my next quarry, I saw other uncollared dragons, among them Niva, Ria, and Amacarin, carrying riders who were leaping with varying degrees of success onto the collared dragons. Many were falling, but the strait was deep and none of the dragons were very high in the air. I saw the riders swimming toward shore, though they were soon picked up by their dragons for a second try.

I noticed one dragon that did not engage our forces. Hovering high above the fight, a dull orange-colored beast hung back and surveyed the scene. There was no wound on him that I could see, although every other dragon in sight had at least a singe mark, if not a gash or patch of missing scales.

"I think that's the Citatian commander," I shouted to Gala, pointing.

She went for him, passing well below and then twisting in midair to come up behind. I stood up and went to her shoulder as I had done with Shardas. The orange dragon and his rider had not noticed us. I grasped my belt knife, took a deep breath, and then leaped across the gap. I landed on the orange dragon's rump and nearly slid off. But then, in my frantic scrambling, I jabbed my knife between two scales. It was purely by accident, but it provided me with a much-needed handhold, while the orange dragon twisted in pain. As soon as I was high enough on his back to take hold of a spine ridge, I pulled my knife free, narrowly avoiding the splash of burning hot blood that came with it, and started to creep up behind the rider.

"Daan oon lang!" the man was shouting at the dragon, beating on its neck with his fist. He hadn't seen me, and no doubt thought his dragon was merely being fractious.

He was very surprised when I sat down behind him and pressed a knife to his throat. I hoped he would surrender: it just wasn't in me to kill a man.

"Nod if you understand me," I said, loud and slow.

He nodded, just as slowly.

"Are you in command?"

He nodded.

"Give the order to surrender."

A tentative shake of the head.

"Surrender," I repeated.

"No. Die for King Nason."

"Nason is mad," I said. "Krashath and Arjas controlled him. Do you understand?"

He hesitated, and I pressed the knife harder against his neck.

"Nason is a prisoner there, in the Roulaini defenses." I gestured over his shoulder and down, to where the humans on the shore swarmed around the sandbags. "Arjas too. You have lost. Stop the battle.

"Do you see those dragons there? The gold and the blue?" I pointed up at Shardas and Velika. "They are the king and queen of the dragons. They have killed Krashath, and are here to free their people. You do not want to make them any angrier than they already are."

A long pause. I tensed my arm, a sick feeling in the pit of my stomach as I thought I might have to use my dagger after all.

Then he nodded.

The Sandbag Throne

I waited until the order had been given and the fighting had stopped before I directed the Citatian commander down to the shore, where the main part of the Roulaini defenses were gathered. Part of me wanted to tell him to order all the dragons uncollared, but the voice of reason spoke up in my head. Many of the dragons—most of them probably—harbored deep grudges against their "masters." Now was not the time to risk another battle.

As we landed on the shore and I slid off the back of the orange dragon, I looked around, searching for my friends. The thought of Marta's wild antics was still making my palms sweat, and I felt sick at the thought that perhaps one of her mad leaps had not gone as she'd planned.

But no, there she was! Tobin was holding her so tightly that her feet weren't touching the ground. The grim look on his face was slowly being replaced by one of pride, as they gathered a circle of Roulaini soldiers, all cheering and trying to pat her on the back.

"It seems we have a new heroine for the Second Dragon War," said a voice behind me.

I whirled around, and Luka caught me up in a fierce hug. He didn't let go until Shardas tried to forcibly separate us.

"I, too, am happy to see that Creel is well," Shardas said when Luka stepped away. "But we have other matters to deal with."

Looking around, I saw to my great embarrassment that there was a crowd of humans and dragons staring at us, including Marta and Tobin, who were giving me matching smug looks. I turned bright red and curtsied awkwardly to the King of Roulain, who was standing just a few paces away.

"Your Majesty," I murmured.

"You are the lady who defeated my uncle and cousin?"

King Rolian was young, perhaps only a couple of years older than I, and handsome in an almost feminine way. He wore a mail shirt that looked like it had actually seen some wear, and there was a half-full quiver of arrows hanging from one hip. Clearly, he was a different sort of person from the previous king and his vain daughter.

"Er, yes, Your Majesty."

He gave me an appraising look. "Then it is no surprise that you are she who stopped this war."

"It was Marta who started leaping off the dragons," I

said. But Marta and Tobin were hanging back, and she clearly had no desire to draw more attention to herself. I didn't, either, but it seemed I had no choice. As usual.

Rolian laughed and smiled at me. "Come, sit and let us talk, Lady Creel. How is your Roulaini?"

"Er, well, it's just Creel. Or, er, Mistress Carlbrun," I stammered, feeling even more awkward.

Taking my arm, Luka said stiffly, "Lady Creel does not speak Roulaini fluently."

"So we will speak Feravelan," Rolian said easily.

"I'm not truly a lady," I began, but Luka squeezed my arm, and Rolian didn't seem to hear.

He went over to a stack of sandbags that had been shaped into a chair. There were other sandbag chairs, in a rough circle. Luka led me to one across from Rolian and sat beside me, gesturing imperiously for the Citatian commander to stand where we could see him.

King Nason occupied one of the chairs, but he was rocking and sucking his fingers and I wasn't sure he knew where he was anymore, or even *who* he was. There was a Roulaini soldier standing guard behind his chair, but the man had an expression of pity on his face.

Lord Arjas was a different matter. He was bound hand and foot, but sat in his makeshift chair like it was a throne. His head high, he glared at me hard enough to burn holes in my skin. I glared back. There were two soldiers standing over him, and it was plain to see that neither of the vizier's guards felt any pity for *him*.

Shardas and Velika leaned in close, their heads hanging above mine, and the Roulaini gave them wary glances. After a moment's awkward silence, King Rolian finally spoke up.

"Ah, Lady Creel, do you think perhaps the dragons could be told to . . . step back?"

I raised my eyebrows. Shardas rumbled deep in his throat, but before he could say anything, I jumped in.

"Do you not know who this is?"

Rolian shook his head, mystified. Tobin and Marta were standing between my chair and Luka's and I heard Marta give a soft snort of laughter. I ignored her.

"King Rolian, please allow me to present His Majesty, Shardas the Gold, king of the dragons. And this is his mate, Velika Azure-Wing, the latest in the direct line of royal females," I said with all suitable pomp. "And if anyone has a right to be here, they do."

To his credit, Rolian covered his surprise well. His eyebrows went up, then back down, and he gave a regal nod to the dragons, who returned it.

"If you will permit us to explain what was behind this attack?" Shardas's voice was diffident, but by no means humble, and he didn't wait for anyone to answer the question before he began.

"My brother, Krashath," he said, "was exiled from Feravel some years ago. Well, perhaps *exiled* is not the correct word. In point of fact we assumed that he was dead. He had tried to take the . . . throne . . . from me and to force Velika into an alliance. We fought, he was grievously injured, and he fled, we assumed to find a place to die.

"I do not know where he hid to recuperate, or where he first began to collect and collar his army, but when he reached Citatie this man"—a claw indicated Lord Arjas—"helped Krashath gain control of King Nason in return for being promised the throne when Krashath's revenge was complete. They plotted to destroy me, and Feravel in the process."

"I see." Rolian steepled his fingers under his chin. "And which of these dragons is your brother . . . Krashath, was it?"

"Krashath is dead," Velika said. "This time it has been made certain. He lies in the courtyard of the palace in Pelletie."

Again Rolian's eyebrows shot up. "And it was you who, ah . . . ?" Unable to finish this question, he just looked at Shardas, who nodded in confirmation.

"But of course," Rolian said. "The army wouldn't know that Krashath was dead." He slapped his knee, clearly just coming to that conclusion. "So you had to come here and try to convince them to stop fighting."

"Precisely," Shardas said.

"So, according to these dragons, King Nason is an innocent victim," Rolian said, rising to his feet and pacing around in front of us.

My own eyebrows flew up at the use of the term

"these dragons." It sounded like he was saying, "these dogs" or "that horse." Luka saw my expression and put a hand on my arm. He gave a small shake of his head, and I held my peace. I glanced up at Velika, and she shot me an amused look. It occurred to me that Rolian could pontificate all he liked, but in the end the dragons would do as they saw fit, and woe betide the human who interfered.

Rolian's pacing had brought him to Nason, who was still gibbering and sucking his fingers. A line of drool hung from his chin, and his face looked puffy and swollen. He might have been simple before, but it was clear that Krashath's death had undone his mind completely. Rolian turned to Arjas.

"And you are the one behind all this?"

"With Krashath, but he's dead," I piped up, unable to control myself. It seemed petty, to keep reminding Shardas of his brother, but I wanted to press home the point that dragons were thinking creatures: they could be evil, just as they could be heroic.

Luka's hand, still on my arm, gave me a little pat, and he gave me a smile. I returned it uneasily. There was something about Rolian's manner now, something in his expression, that said he was about to pass judgment on all of us.

Meanwhile, Lord Arjas refused to reply. He stared into the distance with a lofty expression. One of his guards poked him in the shoulder, but Arjas's expression did not change.

"We have the word of a dragon that you are guilty," Rolian told him. "Do we have the word of a human?" He looked to Luka first, then to me.

Nodding, I said, "Oh, yes, he and Krashath both admitted that they were working together to control the king, and to attack the northern countries. Roulain was to be a necessary casualty, on the way to Feravel and Shardas, though." I felt a little smug at that: Rolian might be in charge of this trial, if that was what it was, but it was *our* country that had been the real target.

"If you will not speak in your defense, I will assume that you have no way to defend yourself," Rolian said to Arjas. He shook his head, puzzled. "Why would you help a dragon overthrow your own king?"

Arjas still did not look at Rolian, but he finally spoke, sneering. "Because when he was done with his vendetta, control of that drooling idiot Nason would pass to me, and I would rule Citatie."

"I see." Rolian walked back to us.

"Prince Luka, Feravel and Roulain will need to send ambassadors to Pelletie, to clean up the mess that is left and see to the succession." He glanced at Nason. "I do not believe that this man is fit to rule now, if he ever was. As your father's representative, do you agree?"

"I do." Luka bowed his head. "Since I was the ambassador to Citatie until very recently, I volunteer myself to stand for Feravel. Of course, we must ask my father's official sanction."

"Of course," Rolian agreed. "I am thinking of send-ing my sister's husband. The Grand Duke Charmion is a man of great intelligence and delicacy," Rolian informed us.

"I am sure my father will have no objections," Luka said.

"And I shall send Niva Saffron-Wing," Shardas said. "To ensure that the Citatian dragons are treated as they should be."

"Ah!" Rolian shook one finger in the air. "Ah! Exactly my next topic. What to do with these dragons?"

"They must be uncollared," I said. "But gently, so that they do not panic." I didn't add that they needed to be uncollared as far from their riders as possible, to avoid a slaughter.

"Is that really wise?" Rolian arched just one eyebrow this time. "They are trained fighters, conditioned to hate northerners, and very clever beasts, it would seem. Is it safe for them to roam around uncollared?"

I half rose out of my seat. Luka's cheeks colored and he opened his mouth to protest. And then Shardas leaned over me so that he was looking Rolian directly in the eye.

"You are surrounded by soldiers, trained to kill and to be loyal to you and Roulain. Is it safe for them to be walking around loose? Should they be collared?" Shardas paused.

I was pleased that Shardas was using the same

argument that I had tried with Earl Sarryck at the start of this mess. It seemed that we thought very much alike.

Continuing on, Shardas said, "Human soldiers do not need restraint to keep them from killing, and neither do dragons. These dragons have been coerced, tortured even, and deserve to be set free.

"We are not a warlike race," he continued. "We do not revel in killing, nor are we hungry for land or power the way most humans seem to be. We *shall* uncollar the Citatian dragons, gently, as Creel suggested. And you will leave the punishing of any dragons to me. I am their king, they are my responsibility. Not yours." He drew back.

"I . . . see," Rolian said, his smooth voice coming perilously close to squeaking. "Very well, then."

"Yes," Shardas said. "Very well." He looked at the two captive Citatians. "You may do with them as you like," he announced. "But now I must aid my people." And he and Velika turned away.

Standing, I gave another small curtsy. It was small because curtsying in my Citatian trousers looked and felt ridiculous. "If you will excuse me, Your Majesty, I would like to go with my friends."

"Ah, hmm, of course, Lady Creel," Rolian said.

As I passed the orange dragon, I caught hold of the collar and gave a little tug. "You, come with me," I told him, not unkindly.

The commander started to protest, but the Roulaini

soldier guarding him raised his halberd in a meaningful way. The Citatian commander subsided, nodding for his dragon to follow me. The Roulaini halberdier gave me a cordial smile, which I returned.

With one hand on the orange dragon's collar, I led him along the shore to where his king and queen were gathering their kind. I saw Niva and Feniul, and all my friends, and waved to them. Niva just nodded, busy organizing the Citatian dragons for their uncollaring. Feniul came slithering across the sand to meet me, though, carrying the proud news that Ria had agreed to be his mate.

"We shall have dogs and monkeys and our very own sheep for eating," he said, his eyes glowing.

"That's wonderful, Feniul." I gave him a kiss on the end of his scaly nose. "Now be a dear and help me get this collar off of Orange, here."

At the Border

The war was over and we were taking our people home at long last.

Niva and Leontes had brought their hatchlings to Citatie, to keep the young ones out of trouble while their parents oversaw the uncollaring of the dragons and made sure that the dragons' needs were being met. Shardas wanted to go himself, but Velika and I had prevailed in our insistence that he return to Feravel and heal. Even with the silk wing covers, his wounds had been reopened by the battles, and it would be some time before he was whole.

Luka had stayed on as well, to accompany the Roulaini ambassador to Citatie. Since the Roulaini had refused to be flown to Pelletie on dragonback, Luka had agreed to travel first by boat and then by horse to the city, which would take days instead of hours. Tobin was with him as bodyguard, which made Marta sigh a great deal. I tried to be sympathetic, and also to hide my own disappointment that Luka and I would be separated yet again.

So it was a rather subdued party that made its way to

Feravel. Dragons that Velika and Shardas knew and cherished had been lost in the battle. They worried, too, that the new king of Citatie might try to continue the plan of using dragons as pack animals or fighters. Many of the dragons in that land had been born into captivity— collared at their hatching. They knew no other way of life. It would be difficult for them to adjust to freedom.

"Another thing that worries me," Shardas said over lunch, "is that so many of us have been exposed to the human eye."

We were sitting in a large meadow to eat our midday meal. The next few hours, even flying slowly as Velika dictated, would take us into Feravel. Off to one side, Feniul was describing Feravel's rolling hills and mild climate to Ria, who hung on his every word. Ruli, chattering in his usual piercing fashion, was leaping from her horns to his while Marta pretended not to care that her pet preferred the dragons.

Amacarin lounged nearby, a smitten look on his face, while Gala's hatchlings cuddled against him to nap. Gala was curled up on his other side, occasionally checking on her little bronze-and-brown brood, as though still not believing her luck that Amacarin had apparently fallen madly in love with her and her four children.

"But isn't it better that humans become accustomed to you again?" I said, resigned. We had had variations of this argument off and on since the war had ended. To my distaste, everyone was calling it the Second Dragon War.

It made me think that people were anticipating a Third or even Fourth Dragon War. My only solace was that Marta was the heroine of this one.

Shardas shook his head. "How can we know this won't happen again? If Milun the First could find one way to control all the dragons for miles around, and Krashath find a different way to control us individually, then it is only a matter of time until someone else tries a third method."

"But this time humans helped to fight Krashath's army," I reminded him. "They *wanted* the dragons uncollared." I held up a hand, seeing where his next argument was coming from. "I know, most of the humans were doing it to prevent their own land from being destroyed. But some of them cared about the dragons, too, like Luka."

"And you," Velika added.

"And me," I agreed.

"Going back into hiding is out of the question now, I suppose," Shardas said, heaving himself to his feet. "But I am intrigued at the idea of raising our own crops and keeping our own animals. Ria has promised to help advise us, and we hope to use some of our hoards to buy the lambs and seeds." He blinked a little and then grunted. "Well, those of us with the means to buy their own supplies."

His hoard had been destroyed by Amalia the year before, and Velika's was long gone, since she had been believed dead for more than a century. I had a little money saved, and I thought that it would be enough to help them start a flock, and plant a few peach trees, but I held my tongue for now. I knew that neither of them would want to take my charity, so I would have to wait and present it later as a gift.

Actually, my brother, Hagen, was not doing too badly raising plums, and I knew that I could have him send me some seedlings as well as cultivation instructions. His real job was maintaining a museum that displayed the hoard that once belonged to Theoradus, a local dragon who had died in the first war. But on the land behind the museum he had planted a small orchard, more out of curiosity than anything else. Everyone in our family, he claimed in his letter to me, had "farming blood." That none of us had ever been successful only meant that we hadn't found the crop the Triune Gods intended us to farm. I had rolled my eyes at this letter, and sent back a tart reply, listing the things our father had tried and failed to farm. What else was left? He, in turn, had sent me a crate of dried plums, plum preserves, and plum wine. No letter, just the fruits of his labors, literally, to jab at my cynicism.

I didn't tell Shardas any of this, of course. At least, not about helping him begin an orchard. I had read him Hagen's letters before, and given him the plum wine to share with Velika. Now I climbed up on Velika's back, and Marta mounted Feniul, and we continued on our way.

Just as I could see the far mountains that rose above Carlieff Town, where I had been born, an arrow whizzed past my ear. Velika swerved and shot higher into the air. There were shouts from the others, and we all circled to talk when the dragons had gone high enough that the arrows could not reach us.

"Who is shooting at us?" Feniul was dithering back and forth in the sky, torn between protecting his queen and protecting his new mate. "Why?"

"Is it the Citatians?" Amacarin's chest swelled with rage and bottled-up fire. "Did they send an advance party that hasn't yet heard the war is over?" He gathered two of Gala's hatchlings under his wings, and she shielded the other two.

"Those uniforms are Feravelan," I said. A sudden realization struck me. "This is the border: they must think *we're* Citatians."

There was a chorus of understanding "ahs," and we decided that Shardas, Velika, and I would go down under a white flag and explain. Marta blushingly gave up the hem of her white shift, which Shardas took from her with grave thanks.

We landed twenty yards from the archers and waited while their commander came over to us. I smiled at him in a friendly way, and introduced myself. I expected surprise and perhaps even recognition: "*That* Mistress Carlbrun?"

But I got neither. The commander bowed curtly and

nodded his head without surprise. He knew who we were, he said, and he was there to enforce the Feravelan border.

"A very noble deed," Shardas replied. "But are you supposed to be keeping out the Citatians or the Feravelans?"

"We are just trying to return to our homes," Velika said. She sounded strained.

"Mistress Carlbrun and any other humans with you are free to return to their homes," the commander said. "But no dragon will be allowed to cross the Feravelan border. Ever again."

He handed me a proclamation, signed and sealed by King Caxel, that said just that. All dragons had been banned from Feravel as of a week previous. The day that the war with Citatie had ended.

"That sneaky little—"

Velika put a claw around my waist and squeezed gently to stop me from saying anything shocking about Caxel. The dragons bowed their heads in acquiescence, Velika heaved me onto her shoulder, and we flew up to meet with the others.

"It's happened, as I feared it might," was all Shardas said. Marta looked confused, but the dragons groaned.

"What will we do now?" Feniul protectively grasped Ria's foreclaws in his own. "Shardas, where can we go?"

The smallest of Gala's hatchlings squeaked in fright, and Amacarin plucked it from the air and put it on his back, his eyes soft with concern.

"We'll go to the King's Seat and try to reason with Caxel," Shardas said, but his voice didn't hold out much hope.

We backtracked until we were out of the archers' sight, then flew into Feravel as high up as the hatchlings could manage. This was tiring for the dragons and the humans, for the air was very thin and cold. It was dark by the time we reached the King's Seat.

What shocked me almost as much as the order from Caxel was the dragons' lack of surprise. It was all Marta and I could talk of.

"Come, Creel," Velika said, listening in. "You are a clever girl. Surely you have seen the signs."

"Well," I admitted, "there is Earl Sarryck." The earl had been campaigning for dragon extermination since we had met almost two years before. "But he's just one man."

"One man who has the ear of one human king," Velika said. "A human king whose kingdom was nearly destroyed by dragons. Twice. Even I can hardly blame him for his dislike of our race."

"But it was never the dragons' fault!"

"True, but if we hadn't been there to be controlled, would either war have come about?"

We traveled the rest of the way in silence.

The New Palace was aglow with torches and we could see archers on the roof. Shardas led the others to a large chapel nearby. He and I knew the flat roof well, and we hid behind the tall square bell towers.

"King Caxel does not have a great deal of faith in his border patrols, does he?" Shardas's voice was dry.

"What are we going to do?" Marta was twisting her fingers in her loose curls.

"Why don't we drop you off at the shop?" I put my arm around her. We were the same age, but sometimes I felt like my experiences had put me years ahead of her. "You can go about business as usual. Remember: only the dragons are banned."

"You can come home, too," Marta reminded me. "But you're not going to, are you?"

I shook my head.

She stepped away from my arm. "Then why do you think I'll turn coward?"

"You know that's not what I meant!"

"I know." She gave me a small smile. "But it's what *I* meant. I'm staying until the bitter end."

"Very noble of both of you, but it won't be necessary," Shardas said. "It's time that I had a talk with King Caxel, since my people do find themselves living in his lands."

"So you're just going to walk up to the palace and knock on the doors, and expect them to not shoot you?" I folded my arms, looking stern.

"I'm going to take that chance, yes," Shardas said.

I flicked a glance at Marta, who nodded. "They'll be much less likely to shoot you if there are two human girls draped around your neck," I told him.

For a long time Shardas and I just looked at each other. Then he looked at Marta, then at Velika, then back at me. He settled into a long coil to sleep.

"We'll go at dawn," he said as he closed his eyes. "Better not wake His Majesty too early."

A Meeting of Kings

A single arrow twanged down to shatter on the cobblestones to the left of Shardas. We heard shouting and scuffling, and I hoped that the archer responsible was being clouted on the head. Marta and I, in our finest riding clothes, stood out like peacocks against Shardas's golden scales, so the man had to have known that we were there.

We were quickly surrounded: by archers, by guards with halberds, and by a crowd of bystanders. Marta waved at them as though she were in a parade, and a few waved back. There were even some cheers, and one man called out thanks to us for "giving them Citaties whut fer." When the king's steward finally made his way out the great front doors and down the steps to meet us, Shardas at last spoke.

"You may tell Caxel that I am come to treat with him on behalf of my people," Shardas said.

"His Majesty doesn't, er, has sent me to say, that is . . . ," the man hedged. He tugged at his livery and turned alternately pink and pale.

"You will tell King Caxel of Feravel that Shardas the Gold, king of the dragons, is here to speak with him," Shardas said. "I shall wait in the Queen's Gardens behind the palace."

Shardas leaped into the air, soared over the New Palace with hardly a flap of his wings, and settled on the fine lawn of the Queen's Gardens. He inhaled deeply and so did I: the roses were in bloom and the air was heady with their perfume.

We could hear the scrambling of the guards as they ran over the roof of the palace to get into position on this side. Marta and I dared to slide down off Shardas's neck, though. There had been too many people in that crowd who had smiled to see the dragon king. If Caxel had Shardas killed now, when it was known that he had come in peace to talk, the public could turn against the human king.

"Ladies, if you will please remove the silk covers from my wings," Shardas said. "I prefer to meet this man as I am."

I winked at Shardas as I started to untie the cords. We had used blue silk to replace the panels that had been ruined during the battle. "And it doesn't hurt to show off the scars you got ridding Caxel of the Roulaini and then the Citatians, does it?"

"No, Creel, it does not." He winked back.

The King of Feravel wisely did not keep the king of the dragons waiting. Caxel appeared only a short time later, his hair still a bit mussed from sleep, but wearing a finely embroidered tunic and polished boots. He was surrounded by a retinue of guards armed with halberds, and lackeys who brought him a chair—a throne, really— and a small table on which they laid a steaming pot of tea, one cup, and a plate of biscuits.

Looking over at Marta with my eyebrows raised, I had to suppress a giggle. An acid remark about how I would also like a cup of tea and a biscuit rested on my tongue but I pressed my lips together. Luka's father was trying to gain the upper hand, which was understandable, but rather futile in the face of a determined dragon.

"Caxel of Feravel," Shardas said, inclining his head. "I do not believe we've been properly introduced. I am called Shardas the Gold, and I am the ruler of all the dragons of this world."

Another giggle almost flew out of me at this. A giggle followed by a cheer. There was something so ridiculous about this meeting, about the idea of a human king trying to forbid a dragon from doing exactly as he pleased. And not just one dragon, but a whole flight of them. I also cheered silently for Shardas's bold statement that he was king of *all* the dragons in the world. Marta brushed the back of my hand, and I saw that she, too, had shining eyes and an expression of repressed glee on her face.

"You can call yourself whatever you like," Caxel barked. "But you'll do it far away from my lands."

"*Your* lands?" Shardas shook his massive, horned

head. "Dragons lived in these hills and caves long before there were humans here. Your family were farmers with aspirations of nobility when King Larios Stump-Tail held court in a hollow hill decorated with gems that your greedy eyes would burn to see." His great voice was grim but without malice.

"Dragons have brought nothing but death and chaos to Feravel since the time of my many-greats-grandfather, Milun the First," Caxel roared back.

I gasped with shock. How dare he speak that name in front of Shardas?!

"Ask yourself this," Shardas replied, perfectly cool. "Did the dragons bring the chaos, or was it humans attempting to meddle with dragons? To control us as though we were oxen? Left to our own, we do no harm to you or your people."

"What about the cattle stolen, the sheep and pigs?" Caxel was red in the face and looked near to apoplexy. One of his nervous servants came forward, fluttering, and offered him a handkerchief. Although his brow was beaded in sweat, Caxel waved it away. "Fields and orchards stripped, and the Triunity alone knows how many price-less treasures have been stolen to appease your strange attraction to luxury."

I found this rather rich, coming from a well-fed man wearing a robe embroidered with gold bullion and rings flashing with precious stones.

"What's the good of the crown sending money to

some poor priests to install a stained glass window, if you're going to come along and pry it out of the frame a week later, hey?"

Shardas bowed his head, and I found myself gaping. I normally thought of King Caxel as a bit of a blusterer, proud and stubborn, but I hadn't really thought of him as clever. I hadn't known that he was aware of Shardas's fondness for stained glass, let alone of the connection between Shardas and the window that had gone missing more than a year back.

"You are a blight on this land," Caxel went on in the face of Shardas's silence. "You take and take, and give nothing in return but war."

By now Shardas's head was so low that his nose nearly touched the grass in front of him. I reached out and put my hand on his scaly cheek. I tried summoning words: angry words, glib words, even profane words, but could think of nothing to take away what King Caxel had said, nothing to comfort Shardas.

Because, at least from the human perspective, what Caxel had said was true.

"My people want only to be left alone," Shardas said at last, his voice low and solemn. "We have plans to raise our own crops and livestock, and perhaps to learn to create our own objects of beauty." He cleared his throat, a strange sound for a dragon, and raised his head a little. "Most of the items in our hoards are things that have been lost or abandoned or were given to us in the years before Milun the First. They were not stolen, but if it would make amends, we are prepared to donate them to the human public, that they might be put on view as Theoradus's hoard has been. I know in the hoards of some of my friends there are tapestries of a style that is no longer made, and priceless antique books that may be of use to you."

"How noble of you to give back our own belongings," Caxel sneered. "And how unsurprising that you claim not to be thieves."

Shardas tensed, and for a moment I thought he might attack Caxel, but in the end he only said again: "We want to be left alone."

"But you cannot be left alone," said another voice, before King Caxel could gather himself.

Looking around, I saw Earl Sarryck, followed by Prince Miles and Lady Isla, coming up the path. They joined our little group, Miles and Isla bowing to both King Caxel and to Shardas.

"I'm sorry, sir," Miles said to Shardas in his grave voice. "But I think part of my father's problem is that you and your people are just so . . . big."

"Too big," barked Sarryck. "Too big, too difficult to control, and far too dangerous."

The sound of that voice was enough to make my toes curl. I had been almost giddy at this meeting with King Caxel, because Caxel, for all his bullheadedness, could sometimes be made to see reason.

Earl Sarryck, on the other hand, was not a man who could be reasoned with.

"They oughtn't to be controlled," Lady Isla protested.

"Then what's to be done with them?" Caxel asked. "I've no interest in an army of dragons, but who knows when another power-hungry alchemist will come along? Before you know it we'll be in the middle of a Third Dragon War."

Sarryck nodded emphatically. "Just my thoughts, Your Majesty."

"Mine as well, Father," Miles said, which made me frown at him. "But I mean this with all due respect, sir," Miles hastened to add to Shardas. "I just mean that, human nature being what it is, I don't think there's any way to keep someone else from trying what Amalia and Krashath did."

"One day you will make a fine king," Sarryck said appraisingly. He gave Shardas a nasty smile. "You're not wanted here, beast. You have until sundown to leave Feravel, or we'll begin shooting. All dragons within the borders of this nation are to be exterminated."

Recognizing the wording of the proclamation we'd seen at the border, I realized who had probably dictated the orders to the king. I glared at Sarryck, willing him to shrivel up and die in the heat of my gaze, but he just glared back.

Miles was shaking his head, though. "That isn't what I meant, Sarryck. We have no right to 'exterminate' thinking creatures. But as long as humans and dragons live cheek-by-jowl, there will be contention. I do think it wise that the dragons withdraw from Feravel, sir." He addressed Shardas respectfully. "Isn't there some other place you could go? Somewhere far away from Feravel and Roulain and Citatie and our muddled politics? A land just for dragons?"

There was a long, long silence. Then Shardas raised his head and looked at King Caxel. Caxel looked away, but Sarryck continued to glare, challenging the gold dragon. Shardas didn't return his look, but turned to Miles.

"One day you *will* be a good king," Shardas said. He extended his foreleg so that Marta and I could scramble up onto his back. He spread his wings, laced with wounds from battles recent and past, and looked at Caxel again.

"My people shall withdraw."

He surged into the sky.

Unpicking Stitches

S omething's very, very wrong, Marta," I said.

Looking over my shoulder Marta tutted at my work. "Yes, something's wrong. Those were supposed to be pansies, but they look like . . . Well, nothing."

I looked at the blobby shape I had embroidered into the hem of one of Lady Isla's gowns. Upside down it might be taken for some sort of purple dog's head, but Marta was right: it wasn't a pansy. I picked up my little stitch-ripping knife and started to remove the stitches.

"You know that's not what I meant, Marta," I said as I worked.

She put down the bolt of silk she had been carrying and spread it out on the cutting table. "I know, Creel, it's just that talking about it will only drive you mad. We haven't heard from Shardas, and that's that."

If Marta hadn't been pale and rather trembly when she said this, I would have been angry with her. But she cared about Shardas and the others, too, and was as worried as I was. She just didn't want to talk about it, and I told myself that I should follow her example.

I tossed aside the gown I was working on and lurched to my feet. "Forgot something," I muttered as I made my way out of our back room and up the stairs to the living quarters above our shop.

Nearly a month ago, after Shardas had agreed that his people would withdraw from Feravel, he had gathered up the other dragons and then taken me and Marta here, to our shop. Depositing us at the front door before an audience of terrified neighbors, he had thanked us for our help and told us not to worry, that he and Velika would keep in touch. Then they had all flown away.

In the weeks that followed, the news was ever more worrisome. The dragons had withdrawn not only from Feravel but also from Roulain and Citatie. I had received a letter from Luka detailing how Shardas and Velika had appeared at the palace in Pelletie, announced to the newly forming human government that their people were leaving, and flown away with the Citatian dragons in their wake. All of them—eggs and hatchlings too young to fly, carried in slings, and even females so close to laying their eggs that they could hardly waddle—had soared off toward the desert.

The basin of water in my bedchamber remained blank. I sent letters to Luka, begging for information, but he had no more to tell. I even wrote to King Rolian, who responded with a friendly letter telling how the same thing had happened there, but giving me no insight as to where the dragons were going.

My first letter to Rolian had opened a floodgate, however, and the Roulaini king had begun writing me other letters, rather admiring ones. Marta and Alle, our assistant, were teasing me about having a second royal suitor. But only halfheartedly, because they could see how upset I was.

Where had the dragons gone?

After checking the basin in my bedchamber without success, I went to my writing desk and penned another note to Luka. It had been two days since I had sent the last one, and I just couldn't bear not to write. On top of my anxiety about Shardas and the others, I missed Luka rather badly. I wanted to talk to him about the dragons, and about other things. It had been so pleasant to stay in the cave in Citatie with him, joking over meals and sharing our concerns, and I missed those times. I was also curious about how things were going in Citatie. They had tracked down a cousin of Nason's to sit on the throne, but Luka worried that "weak minds" seemed to be a family trait. At first I had been anxious to know if the new king would treat the dragons with kindness, but that seemed to be a moot point now.

Stamping a blob of wax with the seal Luka had given me (a needle and pair of scissors crossed) to close the letter, I ducked down the stairs before Marta could catch me and hurried out to the street. We were working all hours to get Isla's gowns finished, for the royal marriage was in two weeks and we also had gowns to finish for the wedding guests. After that, Marta wanted us to concentrate on the clothes for her wedding.

But I had to do this. I trotted up the streets to the New Palace, where a guard who recognized me opened the massive front door with a smile. Inside I was greeted by the kindly steward who had been slipping my letters into the courier pouches destined for Citatie and Luka.

His smile was even wider this time, and with a flourish he handed me a letter with Luka's personal seal on it. He also took my letter to Luka and assured me that it would be sent out in the morning, then showed me to a little bench in an alcove where I could read Luka's letter.

It was news that I had been waiting to hear, yet it was disturbing all the same. A dragon had been sighted, flying high overhead so that arrows fired from the ground could not reach it. The dragon flew over Pelletie in a widening spiral, then out over the olive groves to the west. It was not one that Luka recognized, and the concept that one dragon was different from another was alien to the Citatians, so no one at the palace had been able to identify it either.

And that was all he had to say, other than the very welcome news that he would be leaving for Feravel the day after this writing, to return in time for Miles's wedding festivities. Judging by the date on this letter, he would be more than halfway home, since couriers traveled much faster than royal entourages.

I thanked the steward and hurried back to the shop, where Marta was waiting with another letter. This one had arrived by regular post and was from my "admirer" in Roulain, King Rolian. She and Alle watched and cut fabric while I read it.

He effusively praised my golden braids, my sparkling blue eyes, and my sunlike countenance, et cetera. Then he mentioned, almost in passing, that a dragon had been seen flying lazy circles over the Roulaini countryside. After that the letter degenerated into complaints about the stress of running a prosperous nation, and into musings of how he longed to take a holiday by the sea sometime soon, perhaps with a golden-haired companion at his side.

I tossed the letter aside and told Marta and Alle about the important parts of both letters: that dragons had been seen, alone and flying in circles out of bowshot. What it all meant, we didn't know, but I was so distracted by this news that I not only unpicked my lopsided pansy, but the one next to it as well, which had been perfectly good. I cursed, and forced myself to concentrate on the task at hand, rather than on the thoughts swirling through my brain.

What were the dragons doing?

A Plethora of Princes

No more news came until Marta and I went to the New Palace to make the final adjustments to Isla's gowns. We were ushered into the countess's sitting room by a grinning maid, who smiled wider when we asked her what was so amusing. In the sitting room we found out: Isla was there, and so were Luka and Tobin.

Stepping out of the room, Isla left us to greet them. Marta and Tobin were, of course, quite shameless in their kissing, whereas Luka and I kissed only once and hugged for no more than a count of ten (not that I was counting . . . really) before we stepped apart to cough and say hello. My excitement at seeing him chased thoughts of the dragons from my mind as I asked how his journey had been and when he had arrived back in the King's Seat.

Or, at least, it temporarily chased these thoughts from my mind.

"Have you seen any more dragons circling?" I asked as patiently as I could, after he had told me about the journey.

"Yes, but it was so far away that I wasn't entirely sure. But Tobin assures me that there is no such thing as a purple eagle, so it was mostly likely a dragon." His flippant tone didn't completely hide the concern in his eyes. "And you haven't heard from Shardas?"

"Not a peep," I told him. "Nor from any of the others." I picked at the embroidery on my cuffs. Somehow in my mind, Luka's return had been linked to a return of the dragons, and now I was realizing how foolish that had been.

"Hello, maidies!"

A pale-haired man, grinning broadly, stuck his head into the room just then. For a second, taking in the smiling tanned face and pointed hat, combined with his greeting, I thought it was our old friend the monkey seller. Then he came all the way into the room, and I saw that his hat was royal purple and that he bore a striking resemblance to King Nason.

"Ladies," Luka said, the flash of dismay on his face quickly turning to a polite smile. "Please allow me to introduce Prince Lanon of Citatie. The prince is here as his brother, King Baul's, ambassador." Luka bowed and then swept an arm toward me and Marta. "Prince Lanon, allow me to present Creelisel Carlbrun and Marita Hargady."

"Hello, hello!" He bowed and said something in Citatian that I couldn't catch, but Tobin took a step closer to Marta, and Luka took my hand.

I listened carefully to Luka's reply, and thought I caught the word for "wives." My eyebrows climbed to my hairline, and I gave the foreign prince a quelling look.

"He said that you were both exotic looking, and would make nice wives," Luka said out of the corner of his mouth. "I told him that Marta was betrothed, and that you, well, wouldn't make a nice wife."

"Thanks," I murmured, and elbowed him in the ribs. I thought I would make a very nice wife. Someday.

"He already has fifteen wives, you don't want him to court you," Luka whispered, discreetly rubbing his side where I'd elbowed him.

"Ick," Marta said under her breath.

The Citatian prince continued to grin and nod at us, until finally Luka took him by the elbow and steered him out of the room. They talked in the passageway in Citatian for a little while and then Luka came back in alone.

"Whew!" He blew out his breath. "It seems that Nason isn't the only one in that family who is dumber than two turnips in a rain barrel." He grinned at me. "As your aunt might say."

"Really?" I threw a nervous look after the foreign prince. "What's the new king like?"

"Not as clever as one might hope a king to be. Nor is he as foolish as some in the family, however," Luka said. "He doesn't have any ambitions to conquer other lands or to harness the local dragons for his own gain, so I suppose he'll do just fine."

"Not that there are any dragons around to harness," Marta pointed out.

Further discussion was curtailed by Miles and Isla. They had decided that we had had more than enough time to say hello, and came in to chat. Then we sent the men away while Marta and I got down to the business of dressmaking.

"I'm sure your wedding gown will be divine," Isla said to Marta. Marta, pinning the waist of Isla's gown where it needed to be taken in a pinch, smiled modestly.

"She'll be gorgeous," I confirmed. "Oh, Marta, you know you will! The gown for the Feravelan ceremony has yard after yard after yard of silk, and a stiffened ruff of lace around her throat." Said ruff was currently giving me nightmares as I tried to sew it in such a way that would allow it to stand free with minimal starching and yet not strangle my friend.

"Ooh, heavenly," Isla sighed, and looked into the mirror.

"Don't even think about feeling poor in comparison," I scolded her. "Your gown is even more magificent."

And it was: the yards of white satin that made up the skirt had tiny crystals sewn into the centers of embroidered white flowers. The crystals were inspired by the mirrored silk I'd seen in Citatie, and they gave the gown just a hint of color. Brides "married in the eyes of the Triunity," as we say in Feravel, were required to wear nothing but white from the skin out, and it got to be a bit monotonous. We were currently adding crystals to Marta's Feravelan gown as well, to give her a bit of sparkle. I had a feeling, though, that Marta would never be satisfied with her gown, and that we would be adding tucks and ribbons well after she and Tobin were married and surrounded by children.

We finished the fitting of the wedding gown, and then checked the fit of several others. Tomorrow night would be the start of a week of banquets and balls, culminating in the ceremony itself.

"I'm sorry that I've been so selfish, having you spend all your time on my gowns," Isla said as we helped her back into one of her old gray gowns.

"Well, that is what we do," I said with a shrug. "We're dressmakers."

She laughed. "I know. I just didn't know if you would have enough time to make your own gowns. It's not at all fashionable to wear the same thing twice during the banquet week."

Marta and I exchanged puzzled glances.

"Oh, no!" Isla put a hand to her lips. "Luka didn't tell you, did he? That terrible boy! He probably talked about nothing but dragons and deserts and dogs!" She tapped one foot.

Again, Marta and I looked at each other, and then at our client.

"You're both invited to the wedding," Isla said with a

laugh. "You're Tobin's betrothed," she reminded Marta (as though she needed to be reminded), "and you're such great friends with Luka, and with Miles, Creel. We decided a few days ago that we had to have you both celebrate with us. I thought perhaps you had already been invited, or I would have told you sooner, but I asked Miles and he said no. Tobin and Luka said that they would tell you themselves, and they didn't!" She shook her head. "Those boys!"

I did not think that Tobin, who was practically a giant and tattooed to boot, had been called a "boy" since he was in swaddling clothes. The image of Isla taking Tobin by one pierced ear and giving him a scolding made me laugh. Then I sobered quickly, thinking of my wardrobe and what I might have to wear to a royal wedding.

"Wear it," Marta said out of the corner of her mouth as we gathered up our things.

"What?" I blinked at her as I folded the white satin wedding gown into its linen wrappings.

"Wear it. You know which one. For the ceremony."

I shook back my hair, which I still wore in dozens of tiny braids, some of which were still blue. "I can't think what you mean," I said.

But I did know what she meant. She meant the gold gown I had worn to the Merchants' Ball the night the first Dragon War had begun. It had been some of my finest work, but by the time that horrible night was over, it was ruined. Dirty, stained, sweaty, and with the over-skirt slit front and back to make riding more convenient, it should have been thrown away. But I couldn't bring myself to get rid of it entirely, so I had put it in a trunk and tried to forget.

"I've seen you working on it," Marta whispered. "You can't fool me."

"I just . . . cleaned it," I muttered. "It's still torn up."

"You may come in now," Isla was calling out to Miles and the other men, who had been across the hall sharp-ening knives and talking about hunting, or whatever it is men do when they're alone.

"Don't tell me you couldn't have it mended and glo-rious by the end of the week, Creel, I know you," Marta said. She gave my braids a yank, and went to hold hands with Tobin.

"Hello again, maidy!" Prince Lanon grinned broadly as he came back into the room.

I soon found myself sitting down to tea with the crown prince of Feravel, the younger Prince Luka, Prince Luka's former bodyguard, the countess of Dran-vel, my common-born business partner, and a Citatian prince who seemed determined to make me wife num-ber sixteen.

I would have been self-conscious, but in my mind I kept seeing a swirl of gold silk underskirts, and the daz-zle of satin embroidered with jewel-like colors.

Marta was right: it could be done.

A Royal Wedding

W hat if this gown is cursed?" Alle looked at me with wide eyes.

I looked back at her, also wide-eyed, but mostly from surprise. "You don't honestly believe that a gown can be cursed?"

Alle had been an apprentice with me and Marta before the first war, at Mistress Derda's shop. It had been awkward at first, employing someone who had once been an equal, but Marta and I quickly convinced her that she didn't have to call either of us "mistress," and we stayed friends. Alle was helping me get ready for Isla and Miles's official ceremony, and her eyes had nearly fallen out of her head when she saw the gown I had laid out on the bed.

Even with the changes that I had had to make, there was no mistaking it. It was my gown from the Merchants' Ball, remade into something that I flattered myself was even more stunning. But it carried with it the memories of that night.

Shardas had destroyed the New Palace, caught up in

the force of a pair of dragonskin slippers, which an alchemist had created from Velika's own hide.

Under the orders of Princess Amalia of Roulain, dragons had descended on the King's Seat, burning everything in their path.

Miles had been abducted and held hostage by the Roulaini, while Luka barely managed to escape. Their father had been cornered in the caves beneath the city, fighting for his life. Needless to say, the gown had had a rather dramatic debut.

"I don't have anything else grand enough to wear to a royal wedding," I said quietly. "And it isn't cursed."

I only hoped that the changes made to the gown would be enough to convince the wedding guests that it wasn't cursed. Or even better, that it was a completely different gown.

I had ripped the old underskirts out and replaced them with layers of filmy blue silk, the edges of which I had singed with a candle rather than hemmed. It kept them from fraying and made them look like flower petals. The bodice needed refitting (the bust had to be loosened, much to my secret delight), and I added more abstract embroidery to cover the stitches.

The heavy overskirt, shorter than the underskirts, had a long slit in the front and back that I decided not to mend. Marta had made the cuts, and she had carefully cut between the panels of embroidery to preserve my handiwork. I finished off the edges, leaving the skirt in two broad sections that parted when I walked to show off more of the rich blue silk underneath.

Washing the scarlet sash I had originally worn had resulted in the poor scrap of cloth coming completely unraveled at the ends, and I had thrown it in the rag bag. I took a narrow length of green silk and wound it around my torso from waist to short ribs, tucking in the ends in the Citatian fashion.

"Gah!" I looked in the mirror and put my hands to my face. "I look like a peacock! Take it off!" I reached for the sash, frantically wondering what I could possibly wear instead. During the past week of feasts and dancing, I had worn my only three suitably formal gowns and then had had to resort to borrowing two of Alle's.

"You look like a queen," Alle said.

I had messily bundled my hair up on top of my head with a couple of pins, and now she pulled it down. The multitude of tiny braids I had been wearing had kinked it, possibly permanently, into a wild frisson of straw-gold. That blue Citatian dye was definitely not going to wash out anytime soon. I had been wearing the braids woven into one big plait and wrapped around my head, but Marta had ordered me to wear it in a looser fashion for the ceremony.

Now Alle shook it out, letting it fall around my shoulders and back. It went well past my hips, and in the dry summer air it crackled around me. She used a green ribbon to hold it back from my face, and fastened a gold brooch shaped like a coiled dragon to the ribbon just above my left temple.

The brooch, like all my other jewelry, was a gift from Luka. The necklace that Alle was now handing me had been a good luck gift to wear to the Merchants' Ball. The matching earrings had been a present for my last naming day. The brooch had arrived earlier in the week, a memento from Citatie.

When the jewelry was in place, I took another look at myself. I definitely looked . . . startling. I'm not sure if a queen would dress quite like this. But I certainly did not look like a country girl or a mere shopkeeper.

"You shall quite take the attention from the bride," Alle said with glee. "Not that Lady Isla isn't lovely and deserving of admiration on her wedding day, but you . . ." Her voice trailed away.

Marta bustled into the room and then froze. "Oh, my!" She put a hand to her mouth. In a gown of apricot satin brocaded with gold, she looked radiant and made me feel even odder. But her next words reassured me. "You look magnificent!"

"Are you sure that it's . . . all right for me to wear this?" I bit my lip. Perhaps it was too bold.

Marta came over and joined me at the mirror. Standing side by side, we made quite a pair. With her strawberry-blond curls cascading from gold ribbons and her vibrant, fiery gown we looked very well together.

"Just as long as we stay together," she said with a

laugh. "We won't look too out of place among all the pale pink- and yellow-gowned ladies."

"And I'm sure we'll be at the back," I agreed.

But we weren't.

When we arrived at the Royal Chapel, adjacent to the rebuilt New Palace, we followed a footman all the way up the center aisle to the bench reserved for the royal family. Tobin was already there, along with the Duke and Duchess of Mordrel, who greeted us warmly. Before I could protest that we didn't belong there, a trill of flutes began and we all turned to watch the bridal procession.

First there were the flute players, coming up the aisle with their instruments winking in the jeweled light of the stained glass windows. Then came the lutenists and finally a lone drummer. After him strode King Caxel, who did not look pleased to be taking his place beside me. Luka strode up the aisle next and squeezed between me and his father, much to my relief. Isla's family came after, to sit across the aisle from us, and then the priest led in the happy couple. They were radiant in their white clothes and smiling at each other as if no one else existed.

I thought wistfully that it might be nice one day to have someone look at me like that. Realizing that Luka was staring at me, I gave him a quizzical look, straightening my sash nervously.

"Is my gown too gaudy for the wedding?" I asked as low as I could, and he bent slightly to hear me.

"You look . . . wonderful," he said.

I blushed at the praise and turned my attention to the ceremony, which had just begun. The Ur-priest of all Feravel was performing the ceremony, of course, since it was the crown prince getting married. The aged priest was well into the first prayer, an exhortation that Caxon, the greatest of the Triune gods, smile down on the couple. I did my best to pay attention, and not think about how Luka's hand was very close to my hand, his fingers twitching as though he were going to take my hand.

But then something happened that took my attention off Luka, and off the bride and groom as well. The window at the front of the chapel, behind the altar, went dark. It might have been clouds suddenly obscuring the sun, but it was not yet noon and the sun was streaming through the windows to our left without a hint of shadow.

The light came back but the window was dark again a second later. Glancing around, I saw that I wasn't the only one staring beyond the droning priest at the massive circle of glass behind him. Luka was now gripping my hand in a most unromantic fashion. On my other side Marta was whispering to Tobin and he was pointing discreetly to the front.

"This isn't good," I said under my breath.

"What?" Luka leaned down to listen, but his eyes were fixed on the window.

"I think my gown is cursed," I whispered to him.

With a cracking of wood and a squeal of twisting nails, the front chapel window was pulled from its frame. A dragon bellowed, and the expected crash of breaking glass was replaced with a *whump* and someone swearing "by the First Fires!"

There was not a sound inside the chapel. Even the Ur-priest had stopped to look at what had happened. A dragon head appeared where the window had been, and the wedding guests began to scream and panic.

"Hello," said Feniul cheerily. "I'm sorry about the window. I assumed it would just swing open. Is this a bad time to talk to your king?" He spotted me a beat later. "Creel! Hello! What a lovely gown!"

Parley on the Lawn

F inding that we were in the middle of a rather important wedding ceremony, the dragons at first politely
agreed to wait. But then it was pointed out by Luka that
no one, least of all the white-faced Ur-priest, was paying
attention to the wedding anymore. So King Caxel agreed
to meet with Shardas and Feniul out on the lawn behind
the chapel and hear their news.

Miles and Isla insisted on being included, and so did
Luka and I. Earl Sarryck, who was roaring for the guards
to surround the dragons, followed us without an invitation. Shardas lay on the lawn contemplating the window,
with Feniul at his side fidgeting with his tail.

I ran to Shardas and would have embraced any part
of him I could reach: foreleg, muzzle, tail, but something
in his expression held me back. Feniul bent down, though,
and I stroked his nose.

"Shardas is very angry, isn't he?" I whispered.

"He's very worried," Feniul said in his grating whisper. "We have not had an easy time."

"This is some fine work," Shardas said presently, and

carefully leaned the window against the wall of the chapel. "Merrun, I believe."

"What?" King Caxel looked baffled.

"It looks to be the work of the artisan Merrun," Shardas clarified.

"I really wouldn't know," the king replied, but he did so with rather more tact than he had previously shown around the dragons. I suspected that their withdrawal from Feravel had improved his feelings toward them.

"May we ask why you are here, disrupting my eldest son's wedding?" Caxel sat on the bench that had been brought by one of the footmen, and regarded Shardas and Feniul with a stern eye. "I thought you agreed not to enter Feravel again."

"We are sorry to interrupt the wedding, but we came to speak to you about our exile from human lands," Shardas said. "With guards on the palace rooftop ready to shoot us, we didn't dare wait for the ceremony to finish." He took a deep breath. "In the past weeks my people have been flying over the world, seeking a place to live. We started with the areas that we knew, looking for places that were uninhabited and large enough to accommodate us. But there was nothing on this continent, nor on the southern continent."

"What about the Citatian desert?" Miles spoke up. "Luka tells me that no one lives there. Perhaps the new king will cede the land to the dragons, as reparation for what they did to your people."

"A nice idea," Shardas agreed. "But the parts of the desert that are truly uninhabited—for the Citatians live in all but the most inhospitable areas—are too harsh for even dragons to survive in. We do require water, shelter, and a place to grow our food." His words were not unkind, merely a statement of fact, and Miles nodded thoughtfully.

"I will not cede any of my lands to you," King Caxel said. "I don't care how Milun the First hurt you."

I really came close to punching my king at that moment. His stupid, stout, red face loomed in my sight, and I balled up my right fist without even thinking about it. Luka grabbed my arm, though, before I could step forward, and Isla took my other hand in a tight grip. Her hand was cold and I looked at her. She was pale and there was a dried track from a tear on her cheek. I realized that her beautiful wedding was being put on hold because of all this, and I gave her hand a reassuring squeeze. I wouldn't break her future father-in-law's nose.

At least not today.

Luka did not let go of my other hand, and I didn't try to release his grip.

"I am not asking you to cede anything," Shardas said. "But I am asking you, and all the other human kings, to stop with the lands you currently occupy."

"Meaning?"

King Caxel wasn't the only one confused. I looked at Luka and Miles, and saw a dawning comprehension on their faces, but Isla, Caxel, and I were all in the dark until Shardas continued.

"The Far Isles," Shardas said pointedly. "No human nation has yet laid claim to them, though ships have been dispatched to explore them."

"That's because there's nothing there but rocks," Luka said. "Shardas, sir, surely we can find another place for you."

"Now, son," King Caxel said almost sweetly. "If that is where the dragons want to live, who are we to argue?"

Luka loosened his hold on my hand, and for a second I thought he was going to punch his own father. He steeled himself, though, and turned to Shardas instead.

"Are you certain that you can survive there?"

Shardas nodded courteously. "I would not have gone back on our agreed exile if I were not."

"Dragons are hardy creatures," Feniul said. Then, turning so that the right side of his face was hidden from King Caxel, he winked at me and Luka.

Hope blossomed in my breast. They had found an island that was habitable, perhaps more than one. I controlled my expression, keeping my excitement from showing on my face. It would make King Caxel much happier to think that the dragons were huddling on a barren island, scraping moss off the rocks for food, than that they were living in a paradise that he had given up all rights to.

"Very well, I will not attempt to claim the Far Isles for Feravel," Caxel said with an airy wave of one hand.

"I would like that in writing," Shardas said promptly. "Also, I believe that there are ambassadors here from other human nations: Roulain, Citatie, Nalen, Moralien. I would like their signatures on a document declaring the Far Isles to be the realm of the dragons in perpetuity. And my people require safe passage so that they can collect their belongings from our previous places of abode."

Caxel looked rather aggrieved at this, and I wondered if he had planned on having the dragons' abandoned lairs searched for the treasures Shardas had described at their last meeting. But Caxel sent footmen to summon the ambassadors and a scribe with parchment and ink, while we waited awkwardly in the hot sun.

The first ambassador to arrive was Tobin, with Marta by his side. He was, I was startled to learn, the cousin of the Clan-Chief of Moralien, the closest thing that harsh nation had to a king. Royal weddings in foreign nations with foreign religions did not interest the Moralienins, so Tobin was, by default, his country's representative at Miles's wedding.

He approached Shardas and greeted him formally, with Marta translating his hand signs. After greeting (and being greeted by) the dragons, however, Tobin went on.

"The Clans of Moralien have no argument with dragons," Marta interpreted, her voice clear and carrying. "You will always be welcome on our islands, and may settle on any of them that you like, as long as none of our people are displaced."

I thought that King Caxel's face looked even redder at this. At first I wondered why he would care if the Moralienins welcomed dragons, since the northern sea separated Moralien from Feravel anyway. Then it occurred to me that it made King Caxel's exile of the dragons look even worse.

"We thank you," Shardas said formally to Tobin. "This is an unexpected kindness. Please know that your people will also be welcome in our lands. We hope one day to establish trade with humans, once we have a sur-plus of goods to trade, and look forward to having the mighty ships of Moralien visit our shores."

Tobin bowed and stepped aside to make room for the other ambassadors, who were told of the proposal by Shardas. They all readily agreed: it would solve the "dragon problem" once and for all, and the document was drawn up and signed.

"Now, may we continue with our wedding?" Miles looked around at the assembly with a trace of asperity. At his side, Isla was still looking tearful.

"Please forgive us," Shardas said. "Had we known—"

"Not at all," Miles said briskly. "In fact, forgive *me* for not thinking to invite you." He paused to smile slightly. "As the sovereign of a foreign land, you have every right to attend, or to send an ambassador."

"This is true," Shardas agreed.

"Now that there is a convenient opening in the front of the chapel," Miles went on, "you and Feniul are more than welcome to lounge here on the grounds and observe the ceremony through the, er, window."

"Thank you, Your Highness," Shardas said.

"Yes, thank you!" Feniul beamed at Miles. "And how is dear Azarte?" The dragon had given his dog, Azarte, to Miles, after the first war.

"He's well, fat and happy," Miles said, smiling with more genuine feeling now. "A father many times over."

"Excellent! Pippin is also well. She is soon to be a mother, you know. Being so small, we are expecting only one puppy, perhaps two," Feniul said. Then he . . . blushed.

It was a strange sight. A bright pink tinge colored the edges of his green scales as the blood rushed to his cheeks. He half-lowered his eyelids, looking demure.

"And . . . we think . . . that is, Ria and I . . . we might have eggs . . . within the next year."

"Feniul!" I hugged his foreleg with delight. "You're going to be a father?!"

"Well, yes," he said modestly.

After all that, the royal wedding of Crown Prince Milun to the Countess Isla was almost dull.

A Ring of Islands Like Pearls

After the meeting on the lawn between two dragons and the ambassadors to all neighboring nations, the wedding really was anticlimactic. I felt bad for Isla and Miles, but once they got back into their places before the triple altar, they seemed to forget the interruption and ignore the dragons peering down at them. The Ur-priest, though visibly rattled, managed to conduct the ceremony with all due reverence and at last Miles and Isla were married.

Shardas and Feniul took their leave, saying that they would go to their respective caves to gather any belongings they wanted. They promised to meet me later at my shop, to talk, though this was said with great discretion. King Caxel was wild-eyed enough as it was, and Earl Sarryck was clutching his ornamental sword with white knuckles.

The wedding banquet and subsequent ball, which I otherwise would have enjoyed, seemed interminable. It helped that I got a multitude of compliments on my gown, and on Isla's, which meant that business would be good for at least another year. It also helped that nothing else unexpected happened, thus settling my fears that my gown was cursed.

"You see," Luka said, after hearing about my paranoia, "nothing else has gone wrong, and it's nearly midnight."

"A dragon *did* take a window out of the Royal Chapel," Marta said. "But not for destructive purposes. And it has nothing to do with the gown you're wearing."

"You're just vain," Luka teased, and I threatened to pour my lemonade down the back of his tunic.

He took my goblet away and led me into the figures of a dance, grinning at his father's furious expression while I tried not to stumble. Luka's hand at my waist was sending waves of giddiness through me.

When midnight had come and gone, when the ball was over, when the newly married couple had been danced to their chambers and the musicians' instruments had been put away, I finally left the New Palace. A royal carriage took me and Marta through the darkened streets to our shop, while we dozed on each other's shoulder. But the carriage had to stop at the end of the street because Shardas was completely filling the space in front of Marisel's Fine Dressmaking. The horses snorted and tossed their heads, and the driver swore, making us blink groggily.

"Oh, it's all right," I told him after I peered out the window at Shardas. "We'll go on from here ourselves."

The man had the horses turned around and trotting back to the palace before Marta had even put both feet on the pavement. She stumbled and I caught her, and then we went to greet Shardas. He politely asked if Marta wanted to come with us, but she declined, and so I alone climbed onto his neck and was flown to the familiar chapel roof.

"Why didn't you tell me what you were doing?" As soon as he landed on the roof I sprang off his back and all but shouted the question. "I was worried!"

"I'm sorry, Creel." Shardas's voice had its old, mild tone, but I could sense an undertone of weariness. "These past weeks—"

"Months!"

"This has not been an easy time for me and my people."

This deflated my anger. "I know. I'm sorry."

He swept a coil of tail around, and I sat on it, arranging my skirts. They had held up well despite the dancing and the ride on his back, and I really was quite pleased with this newest incarnation of the gold gown. Now that I was relatively certain that it wasn't cursed.

He sighed heavily. "We had to decide our fate. The fate of an entire race of very large, very diverse creatures. It wasn't easy. We've hidden in the desert, and in the mountains to the north of Feravel." A little huff of laughter. "Yes, we rather violated the exile imposed on us, but where else to go? We couldn't float on the open sea for days on end, and there are precious few places in this world that do not already belong to humans."

"So you found the Far Isles."

"We did. Or rather, Velika did. She, Amacarin, and Gala undertook to explore them."

"So you're going to live on some rocks in the middle of the ocean?" Descriptions from an adventurous duke during the banquet had not painted a pretty picture of the islands.

"Humans give up too easily." Shardas snorted.

"Ahem?" I cleared my throat and twitched my skirts.

"Most humans," he amended. His blue eyes looked down his nose, sly. "There is a ring of very bleak and inhospitable islands, like rough pearls strung on a necklace. But go beyond them and you find . . . paradise." His voice had an almost dreamy quality. "Lush forests, fields of flowers, strange fruit hanging off the trees as far as the eye can see. Wild pigs, beautifully plumed birds— it's a sight that brings joy to the heart."

"Oh!" I slumped down further on the coil of his tail. "So you've found a paradise to live in? I would like very much to see it," I said wistfully. "But I suppose I won't ever." Sudden tears came to my eyes as I realized: this was farewell. For good.

"You *shall* see it," Shardas said decisively. "That is another reason why we returned. We wanted to have it in writing that the islands shall be the domain of the dragons, lest any greedy humans discover our secret. But to our select friends: you, Luka, Marta, Tobin, even Prince Miles and his bride, we wish to extend a special invitation.

"I will be arranging speaking pools throughout the islands and we plan to have speaking pools set up in the human lands. One day, as I told our Moralienin friend earlier, we hope to establish trade. I refuse to give up my stained glass so easily, and most of my people feel the same way. We shall have to do without for a time, but if we can find things to trade: fruits, animals, even our own shed scales and other items of alchemical interest, we might be able to barter for the luxuries we long for."

"But what if someone realizes your secret? Tries to take the islands by force?"

A rattling sigh. "We can fight. There are thousands of us, gathered together, and fighting on our home ground we are formidable, as much as we dislike it. But to avoid that, we will set up a trading post on one of the outer, barren islands."

I caught the idea. "And if you wait a few years before you start selling these fantastical fruits and animals, people will assume that they can be grown only by dragons!"

A rumbling laugh. "Precisely. How are they to know that the seeds aren't part of an ancient legacy of my people?" Another rumble. "It will be a few months before we are settled, and the winter storms will make the flight across the ocean impossible. But in the spring, if you like, I might fetch you for a visit. . . ." He gave me a wistful look.

I threw my arms around his muzzle. "Oh, Shardas! I'd like nothing better!" Then I rooted around in the pockets of the light silk cloak I wore against the evening chill. "Here, I have a present for you. I sent a footman to the shop to fetch it during the banquet." I pulled out a packet wrapped in oilcloth. "A gift for your new home."

"What is it?" He nuzzled it, snorting and sniffing.

"A little something my brother, Hagen, sent me from Carlieff," I said smugly. "Two dozen peach pits ready for planting."

The sudden gust of laughter from the king of the dragons caused the chapel bells to clang once, loudly, and sent up a flock of disgruntled and sleepy pigeons.

Epilogue by the Sea

"Marta must be freezing," I said out of the corner of my mouth. "No shoes in this weather?!"

"And this is the mildest autumn in years," Luka added, trying not to move his lips. "You should come here in the winter."

"No, thank you," I whispered, shivering despite my long fur cloak and fur-lined boots, worn with an embroidered velvet dress.

Marta looked radiant in spite of the temperature, standing on the edge of the promontory in her blue-and-green Moralienin wedding gown. Her feet were bare, and almost purple with cold, but she never shivered. Tobin stood facing her beneath the stone arch that was the symbol of the Moralienin religion. I felt even sorrier for him: he was wearing leather pants and heavy boots, but his chest was bare beneath a harness ornamented with a variety of weapons. The tattoos on his scalp extended down his neck and onto his chest and back. It looked as though an entire clan of blue sea serpents were writhing about him.

"Why are they shoeless and, er, shirtless?" I leaned closer to Luka, not wanting to distract Marta from the recital of her ancestry. She had told it to me at least half a dozen times, but since I had been busy trying to sew not one but two wedding gowns for her and finish Isla's bridal tour wardrobe at the same time, I hadn't given it my full attention.

"The bride says that she comes to her new life with nothing but the gown she made herself—"

I interrupted Luka's lesson to snort at this. Despite her intention to do things just right for her wedding, Marta had started to panic a few weeks ago. She had begged my help on the Moralienin gown, throwing centuries of tradition out the window. I wondered how many other brides had done the same, over the years. Probably quite a few.

"The gown she made herself," he repeated with amusement, "and the bread that she baked as a gift for her new husband's family."

"Please tell me they won't actually eat it," I said, nodding toward the ceremonial loaf in its white linen cloth that Marta held. In Feravel, brides held flowers. Seeing my friend hold her bridal *loaf* was rather odd. "Marta is a terrible cook, and I swear she added a cup of salt instead of a spoonful."

"Ugh. I believe that it is placed on the family's table at the banquet, but I don't know if they'll eat it."

"Let's hope not." I snickered, thinking of the look

on their faces if they tried. "And Tobin? Can't he have a shirt?"

"The groom's vows say that he can offer her only the strength of his arms to protect and watch over her."

"I see."

I glanced up and saw Marta's mother glaring at me. I blushed, embarrassed at being caught talking.

"Creel," Luka said, jabbing me with an elbow, "your turn."

"Oops." I leaped forward to where Tobin and Marta were waiting for me. No wonder her mother had been glaring, I thought, blushing again.

Lifting the wreath of spiky evergreens and small star-shaped white flowers high, I held it out to Tobin. As clearly as I could, I recited in Moralienin the words that I had been told were the traditional welcome of a new son and brother to a family. Since Marta had no sisters to perform this, she had asked me to do it, to my delight. I set the wreath on Tobin's shaved head and stood on tip-toe to kiss him on both cheeks. He grinned at me and I grinned back as I stepped aside.

Tobin's sister, Ulfrid, came forward and solemnly greeted Marta, placing a wreath on her head and kissing her cheeks. She even smiled faintly as she did it, and brushed my hand in a friendly way as we returned to our places.

Putting his arm around my waist, Luka pulled me close as the Moralienin patriarch began the last part of the ceremony. "We should do that," he whispered.

"Wear flowers in our hair?" I was watching the ceremony and not really paying attention to Luka, despite the warmth of his arm.

Tobin's eldest brother, the head of the household since their father's death some years ago, had come forward. Skarpin had surprised us by being as garrulous and emotional as Tobin and Ulfrid were silent and controlled. His red beard was a sharp contrast to his shaved head, and he had six earrings in each ear, a sign that he was a wealthy landowner. He took the loaf of bread from the priest and began the traditional praising of the bride's skills.

"No," Luka said. "We should get married."

Now I gave him my full attention. "What?" My heart started to beat its way out of my chest. "Now? Here?"

"Why not? We can always get married again in Feravel if Father demands it." His eyes sparkled down at me. "Say yes?"

"You're a prince, I'm a dressmaker!"

"You're only a commoner because you choose to be," Luka whispered fiercely. "For everything you've done in the past two years, you could have been awarded a title ten times over! You keep turning them down!"

I hesitated. "I don't think I deserve to be a duchess just because I've managed to survive two wars," I finally said. Then I straightened my spine. "Your father will kill us both! He hates me, my common birth aside!" It was hard for me to keep my voice to a whisper, but I did my best, ignoring Mistress Hargady's glares.

"He does suspect that you started the wars on purpose," Luka said, amused. "But that doesn't matter. I'm a second son; I have more room to maneuver than Miles."

"Maneuver?"

"You know what I mean: to fall in love." A thrill ran through me at his words. He loved me!

Luka pulled me closer. "Say yes."

I was still tingling all over. "I shall have to think about it," I said with mock dignity as I extracted myself from his arms. People were starting to stare. "I *do* have a shop to run."

"I am accounted a fair bookkeeper," Luka said.

"And I have promised to visit the Far Isles next spring to see Shardas and Velika's new home and bring them more seeds and perhaps animals."

"The Far Isles would be a fine destination for a bridal tour."

I tapped my lips, feigning deep thought. All the while my heart continued to pound and the roaring in my ears was preventing me from hearing the patriarch's final words.

"I'll have to see if you look as impressive as Tobin, shirtless and with weapons hanging all over you," I said, but my shaking voice ruined the lightness of my words.

"And I shall have to sample your bread. We all know that sewing a gown is not a problem for you." He cleared his throat, and I was pleased that he looked nervous, too. "Is that a yes?"

"As long as you understand that we'll have to get married out of doors, whether here or in Feravel," I said, squeezing his hands in mine. "After all, the head of my family *is* a dragon."

PRONUNCIATION GUIDE

Alle (Al-*lay*): apprentice dressmaker; friend and employee of Creel

Amacarin (Am-uh-*car*-in): a blue-gray male dragon

Amalia (Ah-*mah*-lee-uh): spoiled Roulaini princess; was once betrothed to Crown Prince Miles

Anranria or **Ria** (An-ran-*ree*-uh or *Ree*-uh): a red female dragon, originally from Luriel

Arjas (*Ah*-ree-ahs): grand vizier of Citatie

Baul (Bawl): a cousin of King Nason

Carlieff (*Cahr*-leef): Creel's hometown

Caxel (*Caks*-ehl): king of Feravel

Citatie; Citatian (Sih-*tah*-tee; Sih-*tah*-tee-an): a desert country to the south of Feravel; one from Citatie

Creel or **Creelisel** (Creel or *Cree*-lee-sehl): a dressmaker

Darrym (Dehr-*eem*): a green and brown male dragon

Derda (*Dur*-duh): a popular dressmaker, now retired

Dranvel (*Drahn*-vel): a county in eastern Feravel

Feniul (*Fen*-yool): a green male dragon; cousin of Shardas

Feravel (*Fair*-uh-vel): Creel's country

Gala (Gah-lah): a bronze female dragon with young hatchlings

Hagen (Hah-gehn): Creel's younger brother; a museum curator and farmer

Isla (*Iz*-luh): Countess of Dranvel and fiancée of Prince Miles

Krashath (Kra-*shath*): a white male dragon; Shardas's brother

Lanon (*Lah*-non): younger brother of Baul; Citatian

Larkin (*Lahrk*-in): a former apprentice of Derda

Luka (*Loo*-kah): the younger son of King Caxel

Luriel (*Luh*-ree-el): a country to the southeast of Citatie

Marisel (*Mehr*-ee-sel): Creel's mother's name

Marta or **Marita** (*Mahr*-tuh or *Mahr*-ee-tah): Creel's business partner and closest friend

Mellelie (Meh-*leh*-lee): a narrow strait between Roulain and Citatie

Milun (My-luhn): ancestor of King Caxel who created the dragonskin slippers; also Luka's older brother, called Miles

Moralien; Moralienin (Mohr-ah-*lee*-ehn; Mohr-ah-lee-*ehn*-in): a northern island nation; one from Moralien

Mordrel (Mohr-*drehl*): the estate and title of a kindly duke and duchess

Nason (*Neh*-sun): king of Citatie

Niva (*Nih*-vuh): a green female dragon with saffron yellow wings

Pelletie (Pehl-*uh*-tee): the capital of Citatie

Rolian (*Roh*-lee-an): young king of Roulain

Roulain; Roulaini (Roo-*layn*; Roo-*layn*-ee): a country to the south and east of Feravel; one from Roulain

Sarryck (*Sair*-ik): an earl and military advisor to King Caxel

Shardas (*Shahr*-dus): king of the dragons

Skarpin (*Skahr*-pihn): Tobin's older brother

Theoradus (Thee-oh-*rah*-dus): a brown male dragon; deceased

Tobin (*Toh*-bin): former bodyguard of Luka; betrothed to Marta; Moralienin

Ulfrid (*Uhl*-freed): Tobin's sister; an innkeeper in the King's Seat

Velika (*Vel*-ih-kuh): the queen of the dragons

ACKNOWLEDGMENTS

For the record, I never meant to write this book.

After I wrote *Dragon Slippers*, I thought I was done. It's funny, because I'm a huge dragon fan. I collect 'em, read any book with a dragon on the cover, but have never had an idea for a dragon book until *Slippers* came along. I wrote it thinking, "This is it, this is my dragon book, my little tribute. The ending is sort of sad, but with a glimmer of hope, and now I'll move on." But my dear editor kept saying things like, "And if you write a follow up . . ." And I would tell her no, there were no plans for that. Then *Slippers* came out, and people (other than my family) read it. Readers wanted to know what happened to Shardas and Creel and Luka, and request after request for a sequel smacked into my e-mail in-box. But I still had no ideas, until one day, while working on something completely different and instant messaging my husband (I am a multitasking queen), he started to bug me about it.

"You know you'll write one."

"Never!"

"Yes, you will."

"No way! It's not like I have any good ideas for one, like Creel and Shardas going to rescue an entire army of collared dragons who . . . Wow! Hey! I need to write that down!"

So here it is, the sequel I never saw coming and that was largely made possible by the usual suspects: my husband, who really puts up with an awful lot; our genius child, whose fondness for Pixar movies and taking almost alarmingly long naps is what provides me with writing time (I dedicated this book to him because I thought, if I were a boy, I would totally want to have a book about dragons fighting to the death dedicated to me!); my dear supportive family who have loudly and proudly promoted my books; friends like Amy Finnegan who read the rough draft and actually liked it; my agent who read the slightly-less-rough draft and also liked it. Thanks, guys, you make it all worthwhile.

Read on for a sneak peek at
Creel's next dragon adventure

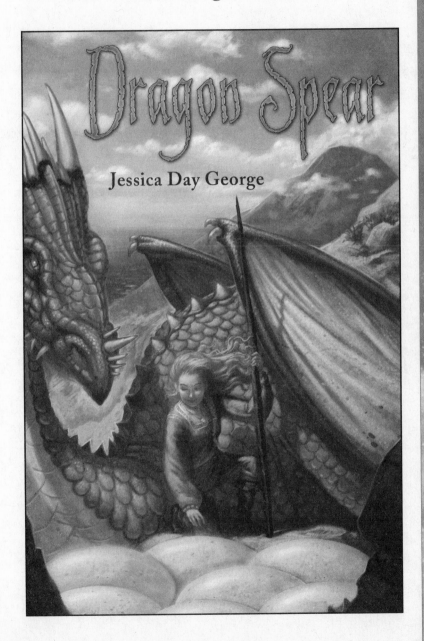

The Islands of the North

I t's a bucket of sand," I said.

"Yes, yes, it is!" Luka was still grinning at me with delight. "*Black* sand. And we got six bucketfuls!"

"How nice," I told him. I looked over at Tobin. "Did he hit his head while you were out exploring?"

The mute warrior grinned and flicked his fingers at me slowly. I had never been as adept at interpreting Tobin's hand signs as Luka or Tobin's wife, Marta, but I caught this message easily enough.

"It's a present for Shardas? Why on earth would a dragon want a bucket of black sand?"

I stepped back from the incoming tide and rolled down the legs of my trousers, then picked up my bucket of crabs. We had been catching crabs to cook for supper when Luka had disappeared with Tobin, to return an hour later with the buckets of coarse, dark sand.

"Creel," Luka said, the pleased expression on his face telling me my prince was about to unspool a grand plan, "do you know how glass is made?"

"Of course," I said, somewhat stung even though I knew that he wasn't trying to make me look foolish. I was very sensitive about my poor schooling: I had grown up on a drought-stricken farm far to the north, and lately large gaps in my education had been brought to my attention by Luka's father, King Caxel. The king was not pleased that his son was marrying a commoner.

A commoner—that is to say, me.

"You, er, make glass by . . ." I trailed off, blushing. "All right: where *does* glass come from?"

Luka put the bucket down beside the others and gave my sandy hand a squeeze. His was equally dirty. "I'd be surprised if you knew; I doubt most people do," he said gently. "Glass-makers are notoriously secretive. Glass is made from sand that has been melted." Now his grin was even wider.

I blinked at him. "How hot does sand have to get before it melts?"

"Very hot. Dragonfire hot, you might say. Shardas has been talking about making his own glass, and the best way to get different colors and textures is to use different types of sand. Black sand is very rare, but it's the only way to make a true red glass."

The buckets of sand now seemed precious rather than strange. I knelt beside one and ran my fingers through the coarse grains. "How wonderful!"

The dragons had been exiled from all but a few civilized lands, forced from their caves and hoards. They had found a new home in the south, on the Far Isles, many days' flight from my home in Feravel, but the last year had not been easy for them.

They had had to excavate new caves, learn to forage for

food, and set up their own gardens and herds of animals. A large number of the dragons had been born into slavery to the army of the desert nation of Citatie, and few of these dragons had even the most basic survival skills.

Shardas, the king of the dragons, was a dear friend of mine. He loved stained glass, and had once had a magnificent hoard of stained glass windows. His mate, Velika, also loved glass, though she preferred finely blown glassware. Both of their hoards had been destroyed some time ago, and the Far Isles were not a place where they could come by either type of glass easily. Which brought us back to Luka's buckets.

I shook the sand off my fingers. "So," I said casually, trying not to reveal further ignorance, "when they say *blown* glass . . ."

"When the sand gets hot enough, it melts together until it's like taffy," Luka explained. "They make vases and goblets by blowing through a pipe with a blob of melted sand on the end, shaping it into whatever you want."

My brow furrowed. "It sounds difficult."

"I'm sure it is," he said, undaunted. "But I think that Shardas is up to the challenge."

"Of course he is," I agreed, feeling a thrill of excitement. In a few weeks we would be going to visit Shardas and Velika and the rest of the dragons on the Far Isles, and I couldn't wait.

"All right, I think I have enough crabs," I said, straightening. "We'd better get them back to Marta before she runs out of firewood."

Marta, my business partner, was waiting farther down the

beach. We were in Moralien, Tobin's birthplace, for Marta and Tobin's One Year Celebration. According to Tobin's brother Skarpin, Moralienin men were so impossible to live with that if their brides didn't kill them by the end of a year there was a month of dancing and feasting. The newlyweds give gifts to their relations and thank them for putting up with them for an entire year. Last year at their wedding Luka had proposed to me, and now at their One Year Celebration he was trying to convince me to get married in Moralien—right then—rather than being married in Feravel later in the spring.

As we cooked the crabs over the driftwood fire that Marta had prepared, Luka tried again. "My father isn't here to glare at you," he wheedled. "It'll be much more enjoyable this way."

This actually gave me pause. Not being glared at by my future father-in-law during my wedding was tempting.

"I don't have my dress with me," I said, firming my resolve. I was a dressmaker, and for a dressmaker to get married in anything less than splendor was probably both a sin and against the law.

He appealed to Marta. "Talk to her, Marta. We've waited a year already, and now we're going to be in the Far Isles for months."

"Oh, no!" I rounded on her, shaking my finger. "I helped you sew *two* wedding gowns, don't you dare try to convince me that one of my traveling gowns will be fine."

Marta sighed. "She has a point." She sat down on a log bench beside Tobin and pulled a fur rug up over her legs. "And Shardas would be crushed if he wasn't there to stand for her family."

"Aha! See!" I poked Luka's nose. "You can wait until the spring." Secretly, I wasn't too keen on the long betrothal either, but if I was going to be married in front of every titled wealthy in Feravel, plus ambassadors from Roulain, Citatie, Moralien, and who knew where else, not to mention the glaring King Caxel, I wanted to make certain that everything was perfect. Getting my dragon friends there was another complication that I still hadn't worked out, and I wished that Marta hadn't said anything about Shardas being there. King Caxel had banned all dragons from Feravel, no exceptions, and I would rather have Shardas at my side than most of my blood relatives.

"I might be dead by then." Luka groaned. He pulled a fur rug over us both as we waited for the crabs to be ready. Even with a roaring fire, Moralien in early autumn was cold.

"You'll be fine," I told him, leaning against his shoulder and tucking my side of the rug around my legs.

"How do you know?" He made his voice sound faint and long-suffering. "It's months away. Anything could happen. Anything!"

The Invasion of the Palace

There really was no way around it: my aunt was dumber than two turnips in a rain barrel.

I'd told Luka and Marta this when I related the story of how three years ago she had decided to leave me for the Carlieff dragon to eat. Which is how I ended up walking to the King's Seat to get work as a dressmaker, befriending several dragons, and wearing a pair of dragonskin slippers that started a war.

But I don't think either of them really believed me.

That is, they didn't believe me until we returned to the King's Seat, fattened on Moralienin crab and spiced honey bread, to find my aunt ensconced in the New Palace, with my uncle and all of my cousins in tow, of course.

Luka was just helping me off my horse when the double doors to the palace swung open and my brother, Hagen, came hurrying out, followed by two of my cousins. I shouted with delight and ran to embrace my little brother, who was now more than a head taller than I.

Hugging my cousins next, whom I now had only benevolent feelings toward since we no longer shared a bed, I exclaimed over how well they looked. Then it hit me that if my cousins had come all the way to the King's Seat, my aunt couldn't be far behind.

"Oh, no!" I let go of my cousin Leesel with dismay. "Hagen, please tell me—"

"Dear, *dear* Creelisel!"

My stomach dropped to my shoes as my dear, *dear* aunt Reena appeared at the top of the broad steps. She was wearing a long, purple gown that even from this distance I could tell was the work of Mistress Lelane, my mother's former dressmaking rival in Carlieff Town. Aunt Reena came fluttering down the steps, her arms spread wide, but stopped with a little shriek just a few paces away.

"What are you wearing?" Her ruddy cheeks went even redder and she yanked the shawl off my cousin Pella's shoulders and tried to wrap it around my waist. Then she looked anxiously around the courtyard to see who else might have seen me wearing trousers.

"Aunt Reena, *Aunt Reena!*" I fended her off as best I could. "My trousers are fine; I've been riding, after all." I straightened my tunic. I had enjoyed wearing trousers in Citatie the year before, and continued to wear them when I went riding, although I'd gotten some shocked looks at first. Marta and our apprentice, Alle, had started wearing them as well, though, and the trend was beginning to spread.

"Well, I can see it's a good thing I've come." She began to drag me toward the palace. "Not just because of your appalling costume, but the steward is being very curt with us. You will need to speak to him firmly. As the only family of a princess, we deserve much finer rooms. Don't worry: I will coach you in what to say. You will be his mistress someday, and he must learn to respect you. Now, about our chambers—"

I dug my heels into the stones of the courtyard. "I am not a princess, and I will not be mistress of the palace one day," I told her as calmly as I could, shaking off her arm. "I am a dressmaker, and I am marrying the king's *second* son. Crown Princess Isla is your official hostess, and *how did you know I was marrying a prince anyway?*"

This last, desperate question was aimed more at my brother, Hagen, the only member of my family I had told of my impending wedding. My parents had died four years ago, and knowing my aunt's aspirations to wealth all too well, I had instructed Hagen not to tell her anything until it was absolutely necessary. After the wedding, perhaps.

Hagen was standing back by Luka, looking sheepish. Luka was wide-eyed, as though he couldn't believe my aunt was real.

I knew exactly how he felt.

"I know it's not until spring, but I ordered some new clothes for the wedding already," Hagen mumbled. "And Master Raslton, the tailor, told Mistress Lelane. . . ."

Groaning, I put a hand over my eyes. Of course my aunt knew. If Mistress Lelane knew, the entire *town* knew. The only thing left was to pray that every neighbor and former schoolmate wouldn't show up at the wedding to help me celebrate.

"This is not the place to discuss your deceitfulness and lack of gratitude, Creelisel," my aunt said, reasserting her grip on my elbow. "Let me help you deal with that steward, and then you will present me to your betrothed and his father.

I hope that five months will be enough time to make all the arrangements for the wedding."

I bit back the question of what exactly I was supposed to be grateful for, and ignored the comment about making arrangements, since they were, fortunately already made. "Well, I would present you to my betrothed, Aunt Reena, but you're walking away from him."

My aunt froze in her tracks and spun around, her face turning as purple as her gown. "Oh, my goodness, I had no idea, Your Highness . . ." She trailed off, faced with a real dilemma. Standing beside Luka, who needed a haircut and was dressed in old riding leathers, was Tobin with his shaved and tattooed head. There were also a couple of grooms nearby whose livery was cleaner than Luka's. Which one was the prince?

I didn't let my aunt suffer long, not wanting to be cruel despite my horror at seeing her here. I took her arm, more gently than she had taken mine, and led her over to Luka. He bowed and kissed her hand and declared himself thrilled to meet my dear aunt at last, covering his astonishment with years of diplomacy lessons. Then I introduced him to my brother and cousins, and Marta and Tobin came forward to greet everyone.

In addition to Pella and Leesel, there were six younger cousins and my long-suffering uncle, who appeared next on the steps of the palace. There was a great deal of hugging, and remarks on how tall everyone had gotten, and then I introduced Luka and my friends again. My uncle pulled me aside during the flutter to whisper in my ear.

"Sorry, Creel, but once she heard the news there was no stopping her."

"It's all right," I said, giving his arm a squeeze. "Really, it's my fault: I should have sent you proper invitations to the wedding." I wrinkled my nose. "I, er, just wasn't prepared for you all to arrive so . . . early."

He hesitated. "No, it's not that. . . . I'm sure I'll be able to talk her out of it by the wedding."

My feeling of alarm reached a crescendo. "Talk her out of what?"

The youngest of my cousins, who had been a babe in arms when last I saw her, raced over and grabbed the ends of my sash. "We gonna live in palace, we gonna live in palace," she sang. "And mawwy pwinces!"

"That," my uncle said with a grimace, "Reena is determined to, er . . ."

He was unable to finish his sentence, but I didn't need him to. My aunt's ultimate dream when she had left me at the dragon's cave had been for the Lord of Carlieff's son to rescue and carry me off to live in their manor—along with my doting family.

I thought I might faint.

Equally dumbstruck, Luka took my arm and led the parade into the palace. As we walked through the doors I whispered to him my aunt's plan to take up permanent residence and he gave a small nod.

"Judging from what you've said about her, I suspected as much," he said. "But don't worry, we can work it out."

"How?"

The answer would have to wait, though, because the steward was waiting for us. A footman came forward to tell us that King Caxel was waiting for Luka in the council chamber, and a maid asked if I would like to have a bath and rest before returning to my shop, and Aunt Reena was pushing me from behind, hissing at me to take all the servants "in hand."

Much to my embarrassment, I simply froze in place. I had only come to the palace in the first place because I had a gift for Princess Isla from the wife of Tobin's clan chief. But now the thought of introducing my family to my disapproving future father-in-law pushed the gift to the back of my mind. I just wanted to run straight to my shop and hide.

I was saved by Isla herself, who came floating down the grand staircase at the far end of the hall in a pale blue gown trimmed with lace—one of my creations, of course. Her smile never faltered as she kissed Luka and me, hugged Marta and Tobin, and welcomed my aunt and uncle and their children as though it were a great honor.

"I'm so sorry that I wasn't here to greet you when you arrived," she said. "But now please let me help you get settled. I understand that the steward has assigned you rooms and it looks like you have changed out of your traveling things. . . . Are the rooms to your liking?" She cocked her head to one side and looked at my aunt.

My jaw dropped as Aunt Reena—the woman who had no qualms about brazenly moving herself into the royal palace— blushed, h'mmmed, and was at a loss for words! My uncle put his arm around his wife, smiled at Isla, and told her that their rooms were perfect, thank you.

"In fact," he continued easily, as his wife continued to gape and stutter in the face of a real royal, "we're still quite tired. I think we'll go have a nice, long rest. Keep the children out from underfoot."

Isla smiled back. "Lovely. The dinner gong will sound in three hours' time, and we can all get to know one another over dinner. Creel, you can use that little room next to my dressing room to bathe and change, because of course you'll want to stay for dinner." She waved cheerfully to the young ones as my uncle led the entire brood away.

I collapsed against Luka with a small moan.

"Steady," he said, putting his arm at my waist to hold me up.

"Creel," Marta said in a faint voice, "I shall never again accuse you of exaggeration."

Tobin signed something to me, and I managed to smile. "You have no idea," I told him.

Jessica Day George is also the author of *Dragon Slippers*, *Dragon Spear*, *Sun and Moon, Ice and Snow*, and *Princess of the Midnight Ball*. Originally from Idaho, she studied at Brigham Young University and tootled around Delaware and New Jersey before settling down in Utah. She had been a movie store clerk, librarian, bookseller, and school office lady before she got her big break. Jessica lives with her husband, their two small (yet clearly brilliant) children, and a five-pound Maltese named Pippin.

www.JessicaDayGeorge.com
www.dragonslippers.net